Emma Leslie

Saxby

A Tale of Old and New England

Emma Leslie

Saxby
A Tale of Old and New England

ISBN/EAN: 9783337026561

Printed in Europe, USA, Canada, Australia, Japan

Cover: Foto ©Andreas Hilbeck / pixelio.de

More available books at **www.hansebooks.com**

SAXBY:

A TALE OF OLD AND NEW ENGLAND.

BY EMMA LESLIE,

AUTHOR OF "AYESHA," "MARGARETHE," "WALTER," ETC.

FOUR ILLUSTRATIONS.

NEW YORK:

PHILLIPS & HUNT.

CINCINNATI:

WALDEN & STOWE.

1880.

PREFACE.

IN this, the fourth volume of the second series of Church History stories, a more familiar period is brought before our readers. The rise of the Puritans was the necessary outcome of the attempt to limit the growth and expansion of the Reformation in the Church of England. The desire for a purer and more simple form of worship had taken deep root in the heart of the people. It was in the same soil that the Reformation commenced its beneficent work, and it was here, and not among the rulers, that it grew and flourished; and its attendant handmaidens, learning and the love of liberty, were cultivated to an extent that alarmed those who looked upon

the *vox populi* as dangerous and sub-
versive of all vested interest both in
Church and State.

This led to a closer union of the two
threatened interests, which at last cul-
minated in the Church lending herself to
enforce the most tyrannical and oppressive edicts of the sovereign, regardless
of religion, while the State, in return for
this, gave the Church almost unlimited
power over the person and property of
the subject. The oppression of all who
did not submit to the dictation of the
Church in things spiritual was a most
natural consequence, and while it drove
thousands of her best and noblest sons
and daughters into exile, it roused the
spirit of other brave, true souls to resist
the tyranny, for the time was passed
when men would tamely submit to be
led like sheep at the will of king or

bishop; and for five and twenty years the slowly-gathered storm raged in Old England, during which the New England was created, that it might be a "refuge for the oppressed;" "the shadow of a great rock in a weary land."

It is this eventful five and twenty years with which our story is occupied, and which of necessity renders it somewhat fragmentary, especially toward the close.

For that portion of it relating to New England I am specially indebted to Palfrey's "New England" and Foster's "Life of Sir Harry Vane, the Younger," one of the early governors of Massachusetts. For the rest, Clarendon, Lingard, Foster, Carlyle, and several other authors, have been laid under contribution.

We can never duly estimate the debt

we owe to these grand old pilgrim fathers, to whom liberty was dearer than life; but let us learn this lesson from their lives, to be true, and brave, and honest in following our convictions of right, never turning to the right or left, whether loss threaten us or the world and its gifts tempt us; so shall we be true children of these noble fathers, and worthily hand down the sacred gift of religious liberty they have bequeathed to us.

Chief Historical Persons.

HAMPDEN,	CUSHMAN,
VANE,	COTTON,
MILTON,	CROMWELL.

CONTENTS.

Illustrations.

SAXBY:

A TALE OF OLD AND NEW ENGLAND.

CHAPTER I.

UNEXPECTED GUESTS.

EVENING was drawing on apace as a party of travelers entered a little village clustered at the foot of the chalky Chiltern Hills in Buckinghamshire. They had evidently ridden some miles by the jaded appearance of their horses, and, as they paused near the blacksmith's forge to make some inquiries, the villagers from the neighboring ale-house improved this opportunity to indulge their curiosity, and make various surmises as to the business that could have brought them to this out-of-the-way village; for Great Kimble did not often see strangers from London.

"I know they come from London, and I know for sure it is Master Hampden they have come to see. Dame Saxby will be at her wit's end for entertainment of such a party,"

said the blacksmith, gazing after the horse-
men.

"Did you notice the handsome green satin
doublet one of them wore?" said his wife,
who had likewise come out to look after the
strangers.

"Leave a woman alone to see the finery,"
laughed a neighbor; "but talking of that green
satin doublet makes me think that he who
wore it comes farther than London. He comes
from beyond seas, and I should like to know
the business that brings him to Great Kimble."

Many others felt the same curiosity, if they
did not so openly express it, and in this they
were not far behind Dame Saxby herself, who
was in no small flutter of surprise and anxiety
at being so suddenly called upon to provide for
such a large party. Half a dozen hungry horse-
men are a considerable addition to supper, and
to one who prided herself on the bountifulness
of her entertainments it was rather vexatious.

"What could have brought them down upon
us in this sudden manner is what I cannot
understand," muttered the dame, as she ordered her serving-maids to bring out all the
loaves in the pantry, and to put down a joint
of meat on the spit lest the cold chine of beef
should not be sufficient.

Her husband, knowing little and caring less about his wife's vexation, was issuing orders for the care of their horses, and expressing his delight at seeing so many friends. Even the stranger from "beyond seas" was made to feel himself included in the hearty welcome; and when they were all seated in the keeping-room, and Master Saxby at liberty to talk to them, while the maids spread the supper on the long oaken table, he gave expression to what was puzzling so many brains just at that moment.

"Now tell us something of the London news. What has brought such a party of noble gentlemen to Great Kimble?"

"Well, Master Saxby, the latest talk among some is the discovery recently made by Dr. William Harvey, that the blood goes racing round our body like as the brook we saw a mile off tumbles down the side of your chalky hills."

Master Saxby laughed. "So you have come to tell me the wild fantasies of a madman," he said.

"Nay, but 'tis no madness, they say; but sober truth, and will work such changes in the curing of bodily ills as the world has never seen."

"So this Dr. Harvey has discovered the old alchemist's secret at last, and will give us an endless life," said their host.

"Few would thank him for that in these times," remarked a sober-looking man, who had not spoken before.

"Well, what do you think of it, Master Shipton?"

"I know but little of the art of leechcraft myself, but I have heard it said by some who are skilled in these things that Dr. Harvey is right, and our blood doth as surely move through our veins as that the king's new Bible is every-where printed and being sold."

Dame Saxby had come in now, and at once exclaimed, "Our blood move! dear heart, the world is getting too wise. Peeping and prying into such things is presumption; nothing but tempting Providence, and I wonder the king does not forbid it."

"Nay, but, good dame, are we not taught that our bodies are the temple of God? and does it not behoove us to learn all we can concerning its mysteries, that this temple be not defiled or made unfit for his habitation?"

"Nay, if God had intended us to know these things he would not have made them mysteries at all. We must beware of witchcraft in

these days, Master Shipton," concluded Dame
Saxby, decisively.

At this moment the host's three sons entered the room. The eldest was a fine, handsome young fellow, about twenty; the youngest, a lad of fourteen, but almost as tall as his
stalwart brother. They were plainly dressed
in homespun cloth; for although Master Saxby was one of the wealthiest men in Buckinghamshire his sons helped on the home farm,
and never thought of despising such homely
work, although a longing to go abroad and see
something of the world had seized Harry, the
eldest.

As soon as the strangers had been introduced the family took their seats at the supper-
table—master and guests at one end, and the
maids and two serving-men below the salt at
the other. The bright pewter plates shone
like silver, and the home-made bread and rich
golden butter, to say nothing of the huge slices
of beef, were enough to tempt a more fastidi-
ous appetite than either of our travelers had.
For a few minutes after grace was said nothing was heard but the clatter of knives and
forks.

When the meal was over Dame Saxby invited her guests to go to the wainscotted parlor,

for she had no notion of her serving-maids wasting the time they might use at their spinning-wheels, or having their heads turned by "London news;" so Master Saxby and his eldest son went with their guests, while Roger went to give a last look at the stables and see that every thing was made secure for the night.

"Now, Master Saxby, we will tell you the cause of our errand," said one, as soon as they were seated in the parlor. "I thought it not well to speak of it before the wenches, for our king is by no means inclined to give such help as many hoped he would to this cause for which our friend, Master Groebel, here has journeyed from Bohemia."

"It is about the affairs of the emperor?" said Master Saxby questioningly.

"It is the cause of freedom and religious liberty," said the stranger warmly, and speaking in very good English, although with a foreign accent. "It is whether we will see our beloved land, our dear Bohemia, and all Germany too, for that matter, handed over as the bond-slaves of Rome, or whether we will cast off the fetters before they are riveted upon us forever."

"Nay, but I thought the electors of Germany had formed an Evangelic Union among themselves to prevent such a thing as this happening," said Master Saxby.

" Yes, they have; but they are not strong enough to do this unaided, while so many stand aloof from them. It is not their fault that Calvinists and the followers of Zwingle are as liable to persecution now from their popish rulers as they were fifty years ago; that none but Lutherans are allowed the free exercise of their religion. The Treaty of Nassau, which raised them from an oppressed party to the possession of equal rights with their neighbors, but likewise prevented others from seceding from the Romish faith unless they would risk the loss of all their earthly possessions, has been as great a trouble to the Lutherans as the Calvinists; but by taking the side of the Emperor Matthias in the late struggle we thought we had secured liberty to all Protestants; but this dream has been rudely dispelled, and we of Bohemia find ourselves in worse case than ever, and the days of Huss and Jerome will be as nothing to what will befall us in the future."

" But I heard that the emperor was about to resign the kingdoms of Bohemia and Hungary to his nephew," said Master Saxby.

2

"He has done this, and our case is so much the worse; for Ferdinand is a tyrant, and trained by the Jesuits to the greatest intolerance of any faith but his own. So we have cast off our allegiance to him, and offered our crown to the Elector Palatine, the husband of the Princess Elizabeth."

"And you have come to England to ask aid of King James?" said Master Saxby.

"All Germany expects it, for is he not the head of the Protestant interest in Europe, and in the new Bible which he has lately caused to be translated is he not called 'Defender of the Faith?'" asked Master Groebel.

His host smiled and shook his head. "Did not this same 'Defender of the Faith' cause to be published the 'Book of Sports' only a few months since? It may be that, coming from beyond seas, you have not yet heard of this;" and, stepping across to a curiously carved cabinet, Master Saxby took out the royal proclamation, or "Declaration to Encourage Recreations and Sports on the Lord's Day." In this proclamation it was announced to be the royal pleasure, "for his good people's recreation, that after the end of the divine service they should not be disturbed, letted, or discharged from any lawful recreations,

such as dancing, either of men or women,
archery for men, leaping, vaulting, or any such
harmless recreations, nor having of May-poles,
Whitsun ales, or Morrice dances, or setting up
of May-poles, or other sports therewith used ;
so as the same may be done in due and con-
venient time without impediment or let of divine service."

But Master Groebel was not so much
shocked at the reading of this royal proclamation as his host expected, for it was only
among those who were striving and struggling
for a purer service in England that the obliga-
tions of the Sabbath were at all regarded.
Among the Protestants of the Continental
countries Sunday, although set apart for divine service, was not kept as a day holy to the
Lord, and so the stranger could not sympathize in the feeling this royal proclamation
had excited in the minds of so many Englishmen.

"I am not one of the Precisians myself. I
go to church, and make the best of things as
they are," said Master Saxby; "but I hold
with the Puritans in this, that if the service in
church is to do us any good—have any effect
upon our every-day life afterward—then these
dances and May-poles and junketings are best

left alone on the Lord's day; otherwise we
had better change the name and call it the
devil's day, for he is most served in these
revels."

"Now that reminds me, Master Saxby, of
my mission," said another of the party. "I
have come to bear these good friends company, and seek the aid of all who love purity
of worship and those who have suffered for
it."

"What now?" asked Master Saxby.

"Well, you have not forgotten that about
ten or twelve years since some of these Precisians went from these parts to take ship for the
Low Countries, where, it was said, they would
have freedom of worship."

"Forget! Shall I ever forget our godly
minister, Master Brown, who was summoned
before the Bishop and cast into prison because
he refused to wear popish finery, to admit
godfathers and godmothers at a child's bap-
tism, and preached the gospel so ably that
half the people in the place became so enam-
ored of the pure, simple service he introduced
as to become Puritans indeed, in heart and
life, as well as in their love of a pure service?"

"Well, it is from these same good neighbors I have heard news of late," said the

guest. "They were farmers here, but there is little of that they can do in Leyden."

"And they want to come back?" said Master Saxby.

"What is the use of their coming back? They could not have liberty to serve God as their conscience dictates even in their own houses. They must go to the parish church and take part in this half-popish service. No, they would fain go to the new colony in America. The Virginia company are favorable to the plan, but as yet the king has not granted them the needful license. Meanwhile Master Cushman here, and Master Carver, whom we left in London, are collecting funds for the last of the journey, and—"

"Right gladly will I help," said Master Saxby, "and to-morrow I will take you all to my worthy neighbor, Master John Hampden, who will likewise give you somewhat, I do not doubt. So you, too, have come from beyond seas, Master Cushman?"

"I have been some weeks in London about this business," answered the guest.

"And how fares it with our countrymen in those strange parts?" asked Master Saxby.

"Poorly enough. You, doubtless, heard of the misfortune that befell them at Boston;

how information had been given to the king and bishops of their intended escape, and how when the men helping to ship their stores and furniture were all on board an alarm was raised that they were about to be seized by the king's messenger. The shipmaster, for fear of trouble to himself, at once weighed anchor, and, the tide serving, put off to sea, leaving nearly all the women and children on shore."

"Ah, I did hear something of a party of women being taken by the king's guard, and they knew not what to do with them, for they were homeless and destitute. But it was months after our friends had left us here, and so I had no thought of it being them."

"These were people from all parts of England, and many of them had died from grief and want before their friends could take ship and return in search of them. This was a great blow to all of us," concluded Cushman.

"Well, well, it seems a pity they could not stay here and wait for better times," said Master Saxby, taking out his snuff-box, and handing it round to the company. Snuff-taking was one of the newest luxuries of the time. Smoking was also coming into fashion, but Master Saxby was not very likely to adopt that. His snuff-box was often forgotten for

days, but he prided himself on not being behind the times. To carry a snuff-box gave
him little inconvenience, and was always handy
to offer a friend.

There was no time for further conversation
now. Dame Saxby had appeared, and that
was the signal that bed-time had come ; so the
guests were shown to their rooms, and Master
Saxby afterward told his wife why they had
come, and of their intended visit to Master
John Hampden in the morning.

CHAPTER II.

A VISIT TO HAMPDEN.

SOON after breakfast the next morning our travelers again mounted their horses, and, as Dame Saxby said she wanted to see her friend, Dame Hampden, about some new method of drying herbs, she also accompanied the party, riding on a pillion behind her husband. There was not much opportunity for talking by the way, but the journey was not a very long one, and they were still within sight of the white chalky hills when they came to the gates leading to Master Hampden's house.

He was one of the largest land-owners in the county, and his mansion bespoke the wealth of which he was possessed. Unlike his neighbor Saxby, who prided himself on his farming, and loved to live in the midst of the old farm buildings, Hampden resided in a handsome mansion, originally built in the early Norman style, but to which various additions had been made by his ancestors. Hampden himself had been improving it lately in the then prevailing

style of architecture—the castellated or Tudor
—so that the friends knew at once, before
they entered the house, that its owner was
not only a man of property, but of taste and
refinement.

The interior of the mansion was even more
handsome than the exterior — the spacious
parlor into which they were shown being
wainscoted with oak, like the floor, which was
polished to a degree that only those used
to walking on polished floors could find any
comfort in. The chairs, tables, and cabinets
were all richly carved; but when John Hampden himself walked in the strangers forgot
their surroundings. He was plainly dressed,
but the calm sweetness of his refined face at
once attracted attention.

His neighbor Saxby evidently looked up to
him as an oracle, young as he was, and Groebel and Cushman saw at once that the success
of their mission in this neighborhood would
depend upon Master Hampden's opinion of it.
Master Saxby himself seemed anxious to know
what he thought about helping the German
Protestants in their struggle; for about the
other matter there could be little doubt what
he would think or do.

" Master Groebel fears they will get little

help from the king, and I have been thinking myself it is a fearsome thing to rise in arms against the rightful sovereign," said Saxby doubtfully.

"It is, good neighbor, and naught could justify it until all other means have been tried," said Hampden.

"But look you, good sirs, your King James has come to the throne by lawful succession; he has not been set over you by the will of another. If your merry England had been handed over to King James as our Bohemia has been given to Ferdinand, would you hesitate to elect another king if he proved a tyrant?"

"God grant we may never be so tried!" said Hampden. "As you say, sir, there is no parallel between the right of King James and your Ferdinand, though it may be he hesitates to help any people to throw off their allegiance to their sovereign, for he has a large belief in the divine right of all kings."

"Yes, yes, but he had better not carry that too far," interrupted Master Saxby; "England will not be held as an estate to be farmed solely for his benefit. He and the bishops are carrying things with a very high hand against these poor Puritans, who only ask to

serve God according to their own conscience."

"And that is every man's natural and divine right," said Hampden. "I will gladly
help our countrymen to take ship to America,
and it may be I can help them to get the
king's consent. I will write to Sir Edwin
Sandys and Sir Robert Maunton, who both
have much influence with the king. I wish I
could help you as easily, Master Groebel.
You want men as well as money to help in
this war, and I do not doubt many will volunteer when they know the cause. I would go
myself, but I am a married man now, and I
know not how soon I may be called to serve
our merry England in another kind of warfare,
hardly less dangerous in these times than a
battle-field, if all be true we hear of."

Dame Saxby had come in to say a word to
her husband about this very business, and
heard what he said.

"God save us, Master Hampden, but the
young men will all be for going if they hear
you favor this German war."

"Nonsense, good dame, the young men are
not so easily led as all that; and many of them
might do worse than helping their neighbors
in this little brush for liberty, I trow."

"'Tis very well for you to talk, Master
Hampden—you have no sons to be caught by
this notion; but my Harry has just gone crazy
over it."

"Our Harry!" exclaimed Master Saxby,
jumping up from his seat. "How know you
this?"

"He came to me this morning, asking that
I would speak to you upon this business, as
he had long wished to go abroad."

"Yes, yes, I know he has; but — but —
Well, we must talk him out of this. He shall
go abroad—shall go to Leyden with Master
Cushman, an he will."

"We can try him; but I fear me it is the
war as much as the going to foreign parts that
makes him desire this; for it was with difficulty I could persuade him to wait until he had
heard Master Hampden's opinion before offering himself to Master Groebel."

"Well, my good friends, I need not tell you
how gladly I should welcome your son as a
volunteer in our cause; but I pledge you my
word to say nothing that can influence him in
this direction."

"Thank you; but I fear our talk last night
has already done the mischief," said Master
Saxby rather ruefully.

"Well, I would not grieve overmuch about it, neighbor Saxby; it will be the making of the young fellow to go abroad and see the world. This will be but a brush, soon over, I doubt not, and then he will come back and settle down for life."

Many, like Master Hampden, thought the same about this struggle in Germany—it would soon be over; and if any one had ventured to tell them that the war they were now commencing would prove one of the longest and fiercest conflicts the world had ever seen, they would have been laughed at as much as Dr. Harvey was for announcing that the blood of our body is not stagnant.

Dame Saxby's entrance had broken up the conversation going on between Hampden and his friends; but they accepted his invitation to stay to dinner, and he took them into the woods surrounding the house, where, through an opening in the range of hills, they had one of the loveliest views spread before them of sunny meadows and leafy dells it is possible to imagine.

Meanwhile Dame Saxby had gone to pour out her grief over the possible loss of her son to Dame Hampden.

The ladies had betaken themselves to a more

plainly furnished room than the gentlemen occupied—a cozy, comfortable room, with broad,
low, cushioned window-seats, as easy as a
modern couch. It was Dame Hampden's own
room, and here stood her work-basket and
spinnet—one of her husband's numerous wedding presents; for they had not long been
married, and the newly-wedded couple loved
this room, and often sat on the broad window-
seats, looking at the trimly-kept flower-beds,
and talking over their plans for the future.

The two ladies sat here now to discuss
housekeeping matters. Bustling Dame Saxby
was not much like her young neighbor, for
Dame Hampden was as gentle and refined as
her husband; but she could esteem the sterling
qualities of the farmer's wife, her mother's old
friend, and was glad to learn the useful lessons
in housewifery which the notable housekeeper
was equally willing to teach.

When Dame Hampden heard that her visitors would stay to dinner, she quietly went to
her larder and pantry to look over her stores;
ordered another haunch to be put down on the
spit and another pie made; gave out what was
necessary for this, and then went back to en-
tertain Dame Saxby, without a word about
the trouble it cost her—a circumstance Dame

Saxby could not help noticing, it was so unlike her own mode of proceeding under similar circumstances; but for which she thought she had ample excuse.

" Ah, Bessie, you know little of the care and trouble of housekeeping," she said, as the young matron took her seat again ; " if ever you should have boys to take up foolish notions, as my Harry has done about this German war, you will not find it easy to take every thing so quietly as you do now."

" Perhaps not ; but I should know, if I had children, I could not keep them with me always ; and I often think my goodman himself may see it his duty to join in the fight that will ensue when the king shall call another Parliament."

" What mean you ? " asked Dame Saxby in a fright. " Will they want my goodman too ? "

Dame Hampden could not help smiling at her friend's consternation. " I know not who may be wanted ; but should he be called to do this service to his country, you would not surely hold him back, would you ? "

" Hold him back ? I could not, I fear, if Master Hampden urged him to go ; but I do hope you will keep him from running into such mischief. I have heard something of the danger of Parliament men, and 'tis almost as bad as going to the war: for, of course, the king is angry when they tell him, as they do, that he must not do this or that. I expect to hear that every Parliament man is ruined with the fines he has to pay, or else that he has put them all into prison. I could not sleep at night, or have one bit of peace through the day, if my goodman went to Parliament; and I hope Master Hampden will never think of it either."

"But he does think of it, and we often talk about it. He says these subsidies being levied and customs imposed at the king's will are undermining our English liberties."

"Well, I don't know. Of course, I grumbled, like every other goodwife, at the duty being put upon currants, for they were dear enough before; but, then, I would rather pay this than that my goodman should go to Parliament to be fined and imprisoned."

"We will hope the king will be more reasonable, and then there will be less danger of this," said Dame Hampden soothingly.

But Dame Saxby would not be coaxed into acquiescence. "I don't see what they want to go at all for," she said peevishly; "A few extra duties on different things, though they are vexing, can never make much difference to you or us either, and so I don't see why Master Hampden should trouble himself to go to Parliament about it. I hope he wont, either."

" He may not have the opportunity, although it is thought by some the king will soon be compelled to summon a Parliament. Master Hampden thinks there ought to be a law compelling this to be done; for 'tis four or five years now since the last Parliament was dissolved. My cousin, Master Oliver Cromwell, who is studying at Lincoln's Inn, was here a few days since, and he says the merchants of London are growing tired of lending the king money, and so a Parliament must be summoned to obtain fresh supplies shortly."

"And you really think Master Hampden will go to be a Parliament man? Why should he take all this trouble? Why can't he stop here and look after his own affairs, and enjoy his books, and this fine house, and all the blessings God has given him?"

"Why, good dame, you surely would not have him forget duty in enjoyment. I know little of such matters myself, but he says, if there is not some resistance made now to the encroachments of the king upon the rights and liberties of the people, they will soon be little

better than his slaves, and the whole realm of
England but an estate to be farmed for the
benefit of the court. He has told me of our
poor neighbors, who were obliged to leave this
parish a few years ago and journey to the Low
Countries, that they might have liberty to worship God more simply and purely than the
king and bishops would allow them here. Can
you wonder that Master Hampden should long
to remedy these things if ever he be called to
help in the noble work?"

"Then you will not try to hold him back?"
said Dame Saxby.

"Nay; how could I? It would be selfish to
do other than help him bear this burden of
duty."

"You! Good dame, you have surely lost
your senses this morning. They do not want
women in the Parliament, I trow!"

"Nay, nay, but women must else help their
lords in other affairs an they are to go with a
quiet mind to the business of the State," said
the lady quickly; and a sudden rosy flush suf-
fused her delicate cheeks as she added, "Perhaps you think these are presumptuous words
from one who knows little beyond the ordering of the house and the tending of poultry."

"Nay, I doubt not you could do any thing

an you willed it, for you are quick at learning, and—and brave, too," said Dame Saxby, with a quivering voice.

At this moment they saw Master Hampden and his guests returning to the house, his young but thoughtful face even more thoughtful and grave as he listened to Master Groebel, who walked by his side. As they entered the house the clock struck twelve, and Dame Saxby glanced down at her tight-laced bodice and silver lace-trimmed skirt, for she knew the summons to dinner would follow immediately.

John Hampden's dining-room, or " keeping-room," was as far superior to her own as the silver plates and dishes on the table were to the Saxby well-scoured pewter ones; but she noted, with something of a grim satisfaction, that the haunch of venison would have been the better for another turn or two on the spit, and her sharp eyes detected that one of the pasties had been slightly burned, occurrences that would have inevitably brought a storm of angry reproaches upon her own serving-maids, but were passed over by Dame Hampden with a whispered word of caution that none of her guests but Dame Saxby was ever aware of. Neither did they see the defects in the dinner, apparently, for they all ate a hearty meal and

did ample justice to the confections that followed, with which even Dame Saxby herself
could find no fault.

Looking round at the handsomely furnished
room, the well-appointed table, and the cup-
board of plate that bespoke the wealth and
refinement of the loving couple that owned all
this, Dame Saxby could not but wonder again
that her young host should think of encount-
ering the perils and dangers of a parliamentary
life. John Hampden was at this time little
more than five and twenty, and seemed to be
one of the happiest of men—one upon whom
fortune had showered some of her richest gifts
—and why he could not be content to gather
these up and leave the rest of the world to
take care of itself was a puzzle Dame Saxby
could not understand. To mind one's own
business was half the fulfillment of the law,
at least according to Dame Saxby's creed, and
that gentle Dame Hampden should talk so
calmly of her goodman rushing into such danger was a marvel that swallowed up all other
thoughts.

At last a horrible suspicion began to creep
into her mind to account for this. There must
be a witch in the neighborhood, who, envious
of the wealth and happiness of the handsome

young couple, had begun to weave her spells around them both in order to work them most direful sorrow and wrong. The thought of these potent machinations and their too-probable success almost made Dame Saxby speechless for a time, and she said but little after dinner until she bade her hostess farewell ; and then she bade " God bless " her with a fervency that made Dame Hampden think she was in full accord with what they had been talking about, and that she would let her son go to serve the Protestant cause in Germany without further opposition.

CHAPTER III.

HARRY SAXBY.

WITH thoughts of witchcraft still in her mind, Dame Saxby rode on behind her husband, silent and absorbed, trying to recall all she had heard concerning several old women in the neighborhood, until her reverie was disturbed by the checking of the horse and her husband exclaiming, " Why, there's Harry coming to meet us ! "

" Harry ! " repeated Dame Saxby, looking up the road, but failing to recognize her own son in the handsomely dressed gentleman approaching them.

The doublet of coarse homespun had been laid aside, and Master Harry Saxby, in doublet of purple broadcloth, short velvet cloak, slashed hose to match, and lace collar, looked every inch a gentleman. He was walking leisurely along the road, and lifted his hat, with its long red feather, as he saw his mother gazing at him.

" Whither away now, Master Harry, in all that finery ? " said his father, reining in his ambling steed, while Dame Saxby could only stare at him in blank amazement for a minute or two.

Harry made some excuse about Roger being old enough to look after the men in his father's absence.

" The callant is not to be trusted," said his mother sharply, " and, besides, there is no Morrice dancing or junketing to-day, and so—"

" I have not cared so much for the junketings of late that you need begrudge me this holiday," said Harry in a tone of some defiance.

" But wherefore take the holiday to-day, my boy ? " said his father, wondering what could have happened to make his son forget all at once the reverence due to his parents.

Dame Saxby herself was so astonished that she could not say a word until her son, blushing at his own temerity, said, " I am going to talk to Master John Hampden about various matters. You will not leave us until to-morrow ? " he said, turning quickly toward Master Groebel, who stood at a little distance.

" Harry, Harry, don't go ; the Hampdens are bewitched. I know they are," said Dame Saxby in a fearful whisper.

Her husband turned round in his saddle and looked at her. " How now, dame ? was the wine too strong for your weak woman's head, or is it the sun and that warm hood?"

"I have tasted wine before to-day, and as for the hood, I have worn it these two years, John Saxby, and know well what I am saying."

"But, my mother, you cannot surely mean that Master Hampden is really bewitched—is he ill?"

"No, no; as well as ever I saw him," said the father. "This is but a fantasie, dame. Has Dame Hampden been telling you any village gossip?"

"We never talk about village gossip," said Dame Saxby loftily. "Help me down, Harry, for it's true enough, what I tell you. The Hampdens are bewitched, and I'll tell you all about it as we walk home."

Harry Saxby looked disconcerted, but what could he do but turn back with his mother, whom he began to think was herself bewitched, or something nearly akin to it, to propose telling him "all about it"—a concession to his manhood never made before?

But when her husband and his guests had rode on, Dame Saxby hardly knew how to begin her recital of what she had heard from Dame Hampden, so as to enforce upon Harry the duty of staying at home to look after the farm, as his father had always done ; and so she hurried over what she had learned concerning the probability of Master Hampden going to Parliament, and impressed upon him the necessity of keeping out of the way of all bewitched persons.

Harry Saxby was quite sensible of the danger of falling under such spells, for the belief in witchcraft was very deep and very general; and though he had once tried to save a poor old woman from being drowned, he was more than half ashamed of it as a sort of weakness that ought to be trampled down where witches were concerned. But still, although fully alive to the danger his mother feared for their friends, he was far more deeply impressed by the fact that Master Hampden should think it his duty to leave his home and family to serve his country; and he said promptly, " Then, my mother, I am sure it is my duty to serve the cause of God and true religion by going with this Master Groebel."

" Go to the wars? But these people are nothing to us, Harry. Master Hampden would serve his own countrymen, but not these Germans."

" But they are Protestants, trying to save themselves from the pope, and so we ought to help them—I must help them," he added, decisively.

"Nonsense, Harry. What can it matter to you about these people? Of course we should be sorry if the pope got the better of them; but then he wont, I'm sure."

"But I am not so sure," said Harry. "And I want to do my part to prevent it. Look you, mother, I've never forgotten about the people that went away from here years ago—the Precisians or Puritans, as people call them. I was only a little boy then, but I remember wishing I could go and fight the king, or whoever it was that turned the ministers out and would not let them even have preaching in their own houses; I've wished it on and off ever since, I think; and when I've been practicing single stick and archery I've thought if ever I had the chance of fighting a real foe—if ever such times should come back to England as I heard grandfather talk about, when they burned people at the stake for not owning the pope—well, mother, I've often thought I should fight for my rights first if they burned me afterward."

Dame Saxby looked up at her fine, handsome son, half in admiration, half in astonishment at such a bold avowal; but it would not do to let him think she was any thing but displeased. "Hush, hush, Harry, you must not talk of fighting for your rights. The blessed martyrs, who were ready to die rather than deny the Lord Jesus Christ, never thought of fighting for their rights as you call it."

"Perhaps not; perhaps they hardly knew whether they had any; but we are learning that lesson in these days, and I mean to teach the pope and emperor that an Englishman is ready to fight for his own or another man's, especially when they are rights of conscience."

"Harry, Harry, I believe you are bewitched yourself," said Dame Saxby in a voice of pain, for she began to see how useless it would be to try and keep this her darling son in the old nest any longer.

When they reached home they found their three guests, Groebel, Cushman, and Shipton, seated in the wainscoted parlor, while their three attendants had gone to the orchard with Roger.

"Mother, you have told my father of my desire to go to the wars—what said he?" asked the young man in a whisper as they paused for a moment in the rustic porch.

"I hardly know now. But, my boy—"

"Mother," interrupted the young man, "if

I had died of the plague you would say God had taken me. Now I just want you to give me to him, or lend me for a little while; for I promise you I will come home again as soon as the war is over; and Master Groebel hopes that when once the Elector Palatine is firmly seated on the throne of Bohemia the Protestant cause will be so strong that there will be no need of any further help from England."

"Yes, yes, but suppose the Elector should fail; what then, my boy?"

Harry could only shake his head. "I don't know what the Protestants would do then; but I don't suppose the cause would be hopeless. God would never let Luther's work be swept away from Germany. We owe these Protestants a debt, mother. We received much light and truth from them, and I think God would have us pay it now by helping them in their struggle to maintain this truth against all the Catholic powers of Europe. The king ought to do it—his own daughter will be made queen of Bohemia; but if he wont, then the people must do what they can, and I will be one of them."

It seemed useless to argue with the young man, his mind was so set upon this; but Dame Saxby resolved to try once more.

" Harry, this place is dull for you after being at college. I will speak to your father presently, and you shall go back to Cambridge. You are strong now, and may not catch the plague, even if it should break out there again, or at least you could come home as soon as it made its appearance. I will not oppose your going to college any longer, my boy," for Dame Saxby had firmly set her face against this since her darling had so nearly died of the pestilence about a twelvemonth before. But Cambridge was nearer than Germany, and learning, even with the risk of catching the plague, was not so dangerous as fighting; so she almost besought her son to return there.

But Harry shook his head. " I am more fit for a soldier than a scholar, my mother," he said; " and this strong right arm can deal trusty blows at the Papists and all who would trample out the light of God's truth. Say you will give me to God's service—to fight in this war for truth and liberty," pleaded Harry.

" Well, if I must, I must; but are you sure there is not some unholy spell upon you to make you wish for this thing?"

"You fear that I too am bewitched. Be easy, my mother; these thoughts, as I tell you, have long been working in my mind, and

Master Groebel's words did but fan them into a flame of burning desire."

Dame Saxby could not stay longer talking, for her maids had already been left too long to their own devices; and, after taking off her hood and changing her dress, she went through the kitchen and pantry, dairy and cheese room, scolding pretty freely all around.

The maids saw at once that something had happened to disturb their mistress, and were not long in guessing where the trouble lay.

"The young master is all for leaving home again, I know," said Deb, the cook, who had come to live at the farm first as nurse-girl to carry Master Harry about when he was a baby.

"Then Roger and Lawrence will get things all their own way if he should go," said Sally, the dairy-maid.

"I don't know. The master wont give things up to them as he has done to Master Harry lately, for the land will never be theirs; and why they should be so jealous of their brother's having something to do with what will one day be his own I cannot understand. Master Roger is the worst, that is certain, and leads Master Lawrence to tease and vex his brother."

"Can this be driving him away from home, do you think?" said Sally in a whisper.

"What next will you get into your head, Sally? No, no, Larry is but a tiresome boy, fond of mischief and fond of Roger, and since he sees it pleases Roger for him to vex Master Harry he often does it."

"Then you don't think they really dislike him?" said Sally.

"Dislike him! why should they? Isn't he the kindest-hearted gentleman in Great Kimble? No, no, Sally, it's just a little bit of jealousy that will wear off by and by, and I dare say they will be as sorry as any body that he is going away."

"Well, well, I am glad you think so. I've sometimes thought if ever Master Roger had the chance of doing his brother an ill turn he would, and I'm older and have seen more of the world than you, Deb."

"But you haven't seen so much of the Saxbies as I have. I've lived with them girl and woman nigh upon twenty years, and though the mistress is sharp, and master, too, for that matter, sometimes, it isn't in the Saxby nature to bear grudges; they are honest and upright, and would not wrong either friend or foe."

"Yes, yes, I know all this, Deb, but still I

cannot feel so sure about Master Roger, and you'll remember my words one day, perhaps."

But Deb shook her head incredulously as she turned to the preparation of supper. " I know the Saxbies," she said in conclusion.

Meanwhile the conference in the parlor had been joined by Harry, anxious to close the matter now that his mother had been so far won over.

It was not so difficult to persuade his father, especially since the talk that he had had with John Hampden had convinced him that England ought to assist the struggling cause of Protestantism on the Continent; and so, before supper was served, the matter was so far settled that Harry and his father were to journey to London the next day to make some further inquiries among old friends, and make the needful preparations if the result of their inquiries proved satisfactory.

Roger and Lawrence were greatly surprised when they heard that their oldest brother was about to leave home, and more so when they knew where he was going; but the discipline of those days prevented them from expressing more than ordinary astonishment in the presence of their parents.

When supper was over, however, and they

were at liberty to wander about for an hour by themselves, or join in any boyish game that might please them, Roger drew his brother aside to where they were out of hearing, and then gave vent to his feelings of passionate jealousy.

"Isn't it a shame!" he exclaimed. "He cares no more for the land than that cow, and yet he is to go off to foreign parts beyond the sea for as long as he pleases, while we work at home to keep his property in order."

"But it isn't his yet, Roger," said the younger brother; "my father may, and will, I hope, live a good many years yet, and the land wont be Harry's until—I say, what bird is that just over the orchard?"

"O, bother the birds! I know this land wont come to Harry while my father lives, but then, who can tell how long that. may be, and then what is to become of us? I wont stop here and work with Harry for my master."

"I shouldn't think he'd want you," said Larry. "I know what I mean to do by and by. I shall go to London and learn to be a lawyer, like Oliver Cromwell, and you shall come with me. We shall always stick together, you know," he added warmly.

4

"No fear of that, Larry; but I can't be a lawyer. I hate the sight of books. Give me land before any thing else, and this is the land I want, and will have, if I can get it," he concluded in a determined tone.

"I do believe you care for it more than Harry does, and it is a shame you can't have it, but—"

"Care for it," interrupted Roger impetuously; "he does not care one of the new copper coins what becomes of the old place, or else he would not go off on this fool's errand. Going to fight for truth and right? Was ever such a thing heard of, and leave such a patrimony as this!"

"Well, you need not be so angry about his going off to the wars. You know if he should get killed the land would be yours then. If I came next, and it was mine, perhaps you would want to send me off in my turn; but there's no fear of that, is there?"

"No, Larry, I should never want you out of the way," said Roger slowly, and laying his hand on his younger brother's shoulder, "if— if this should be—I'm not saying I wish it, you know—"

"Of course, nobody could do that," said Larry quickly.

" Of course not. But if it should happen, then we would share the land between us, share and share alike, you know."

" I don't know that I should want it," said Larry, indifferently ; " at any rate, it isn't very likely to be yours," he concluded, and, growing tired of the topic, he swung himself up into a wide-spreading beech-tree standing near, and left his brother to ponder over the question that had been raised as to the probability of his elder brother never returning to claim the family inheritance.

CHAPTER IV.

BAD NEWS.

HARRY SAXBY went to the wars with many another brave young Englishman. Altogether an army of about four thousand was raised, but the king still withheld his support, and was particularly friendly with Spain, who, with the Emperor of Germany, was the bitter enemy of the struggling Protestants.

Master Saxby returned from his visit to London in no very amiable mood, for, like the rest of his countrymen, he was dissatisfied and disappointed that the king should openly favor the Roman Catholic powers of Europe instead of helping the struggling Protestant cause; but, dissatisfied as he might feel, he had received so many warnings and seen so many examples of the cruelty of the Starchamber, that he dare not vent his feelings in words, or say what he thought of the king and his favorite, Sir George Villiers.

Safely shut in his own wainscoted parlor, however, with only his wife to listen, he could indulge in a little grumbling without fear of arrest. He was securely seated before he began: "I know not what is coming to this England of ours when a man cannot open his mouth to say what he thinks for fear of being haled to the Fleet or the Gate-house. Things are getting worse and worse, dame, and some say the king meant to bring back papistry, with himself for the pope."

"What nonsense are you talking! the king is a Protestant, or he would never have had the Bible set forth in the manner he has," said Dame Saxby quickly.

"Ah, dame, if you had been to London and heard of the doings at court you would not set so great store by the king's share in that business. It is well known, too, that a marriage is to take place between Prince Charles and the King of Spain's daughter. The king is all cock-a-hoop over it."

"Well, and why shouldn't he look out for a good wife for the prince? I'm sure I wish there had been some maiden here we could have asked to be wife to Harry, and then he wouldn't have gone off to the wars;" and Dame Saxby heaved a deep sigh as she spoke.

"Harry will choose a wife for himself, I

doubt not, in good time. But about this Spanish marriage people are nodding and whispering together, though few dare to speak out what they think."

"Well, what do you think about it?" said his wife.

"That England's honor is sold to please the Spaniards. This is the bribe held out to keep the king from helping his son-in-law and the Protestants of Germany. People are muttering and grumbling in such a way that the king must hear of it soon in spite of the terror of the Star-chamber and Sir George Villiers, who favors this Spanish match." ·

"People had better mind their own business," said the dame sharply.

"It is the people's business, dame; for if Prince Charles marries a Catholic we shall have a Papist for a queen by and by, and all the laws that have been passed to keep them from having any power here again will be set aside, and the whole kingdom be gradually brought back to the power of the pope."

"Well, now, you have not told me all about Harry. I have been thinking more about him than any thing else lately," said Dame Saxby with a sigh.

"Of course, and the lad was often thinking

of y ɔu. 'Tell my mother this,' and 'I forgot to tell mother that,' I heard half a dozen times a day, and, I dare say, I shall think of all these messages by degrees, but the din and the bustle of London and the wonderful things so constantly to be seen there have put every thing else out of my head."

" Every thing but the court gossip," said Dame Saxby in a complaining tone.

' Nay, nay, but people cannot help talking about the wanton doings of the court when it touches them so nearly. It is but lately that another duty has been laid upon currants."

" Another duty ! " exclaimed the dame.

" Aye., five shillings on the hundred weight more, and no abatement of the last. The housewives of London are grumbling as well as the merchants, but how it can be altered is a puzzle to the wisest among them."

" But surely the king could alter it ! exclaimed Dame Saxby angrily.

" The king ! what can he do? He is more pressed for money than we are. Knighthood and every honor and every office is bought. Often those who have paid a good round sum for an office under the Crown cannot get their salaries, and can only support themselves by bribes and stealings. It is whispered that the

Lord Bacon, one of the noblest and most learned philosophers the world has ever seen, is not above taking a bribe, although he will not suffer it to divert the course of justice. Then there are the king's favorites to be provided for—the Buckinghams and Somersets; and so, although they are never seen in it openly, they have much of the profit from different monopolies. I tried to get some silver lace to broider your petticoat, but, owing to this same monopoly by which Buckingham and his brother are greatly enriched, the price is three times what it was when I last went to London; and, what is worse, the thread is of brass instead of silver."

"But you could have gone to some other merchant," said Dame Saxby rather tartly; for this was the secret cause of her ill-humor. Never before had her good man gone on a journey to London without bringing her a supply of silver lace for trimming her petticoat and bodice.

"True, I might have gone to another merchant; but how much should I be the better for that, seeing they must all buy of the same maker, and this maker sells but brass instead of silver?"

"Dear heart, what is the world coming to

when honest folks cannot buy a bit of silver lace!" said Dame Saxby. This touched her more nearly even than the increased duty on currants, for she took no small pride in the trimming of her petticoats and bodices, as well as her husband's best cloak and doublet. It was Dame Saxby's one weak point, and to be deprived of her accustomed present of finery from London caused her almost as much vexation as the departure of her eldest son. "And where shall I get the lace, since it cannot be bought in London?" said the dame, thinking sadly of her frayed, tarnished trimmings, and how much they needed replacing.

"Silver lace is not to be had, dame, and the rubbish they sell now injures the fingers of those who make it; therefore I hold that none should wear it."

"But what am I to do?" she demanded sharply. "My cloth petticoat is now in such ill condition that—"

"There is plenty of cloth to be had, dame; make a new one of fine broad-cloth an ye will."

"But no trimmings? It will be little better than Deb's or Sally's, fine as it may be. I wonder what Dame Hampden will say to this? What other duties are there besides?"

"Six and eightpence has been levied on every pound of tobacco, over and above the other duty; and this by proclamation only, without warrant of Parliament, which is making men wag their tongues in spite of the Star-chamber and the King's Bench."

"Well, if things are to be like this, it needs somebody to speak up and tell the king what injustice is done. They would not dare to trim his doublets with this rubbish they call silver lace, and, doubtless, he knows nothing of how his loyal subjects are made to suffer in this matter. I will go and see young Dame Hampden to-morrow," concluded the angry lady as she left the room to look after her maids.

The visit to Dame Hampden was not productive of much comfort to Dame Saxby. That lady had heard of the new monopoly upon the manufacture of gold and silver thread, and she and her husband had been talking the matter over in all its bearings, and they had come to the conclusion not to wear any of this new silver lace, both on account of its inferior quality and the injury it inflicted upon those engaged in its manufacture, and also because of the illegal way in which the duty upon it was imposed.

" Dear heart! and your mother and I, when we were girls together, never thought of how much silver lace we spoiled. Well, I must try cleaning and mending once more ; but 'tis very hard, and I hope this monopoly will soon be put down. Master Hampden must see to this matter, if he is to go to Parliament—and you think he will ? "

" Yes, dear dame, we often talk of it. He is sure it is his duty, and I feel the same about it. You must come and see me very often when he goes to London, unless I should go with him. My mother is very glad to know we are such near neighbors and such good friends," said the young matron.

" Yes, yes, to be sure ; but have you been about the village here — about Hampden ? Are there any old women here?" for Dame Saxby was thinking of the witchcraft that must have been practiced upon her young friend to make her willing to forego her husband's society so soon after their marriage.

Young Dame Hampden looked at her friend, wondering what she could be thinking of. " Old women ! " she repeated. " There are about a dozen who come to the buttery for their daily dole of bread and meat and ale."

"And—and have you ever offended any of these, Bessie?" asked her friend anxiously.

"What can you mean, good dame?" said the lady, now growing vaguely apprehensive; "what is it you fear?"

"Witchcraft!" whispered Dame Saxby.

The lady started and turned pale at the dreadful word. "What has happened? What have you heard?" she asked.

"Nothing, my dear, but what you have told me. But I fear you have offended some of these old women, and they are determined to work you some great trouble."

"But what could they do, poor helpless old creatures? They are entirely dependent upon my husband's bounty, and why should they seek to hurt him? How could they do it?"

"By sending him to Parliament. I would not go within a dozen miles of that Parliament house an I were Master Hampden; for my good man tells me things be grown to such a pitch in London now that a man dare not open his mouth to complain of the greatest injustice for fear of being haled before the Star Chamber. He saw one man taken for no greater offense than saying his father had been ruined through the unjust judgment of the council; and when he tried to escape, the tipstaffs with their long hooked poles caught him and dragged him along like a beast to the shambles. He saw another who, to hide the cruelty practiced upon him, must, forsooth, always wear a mask, for his nose had been laid open and but ill joined together, and his cheeks branded, and this for some religious tract he had written about the right of every man to liberty of conscience. Now, if Mr. Hampden should ever take up these notions, and speak of them, think what would happen!"

"Well, dear dame, I have thought of it, and the danger he will incur; but it is these very things that make it an Englishman's duty to try and get the laws enforced or amended, and even remind the king that he is called to govern the people for their good, not oppress them for his own benefit and the enrichment of his favorites."

"Ah, if some one could only tell the king just how things are going on! But a little while ago it was my Lord of Somerset who kept every one from the king, and now it is said the Duke of Buckingham is doing the same thing; and so I fear me it will only bring trouble to both of ye, an Master Hampden goes to Parliament," said Dame Saxby with a sigh.

"And you think it is witchcraft that has made him wish to go to Parliament?" said young Dame Hampden, feeling much relieved now that she knew the extent of her friend's fears for them.

"What can it be but witchcraft? These troubles can never touch you, Bessie."

"We cannot tell that, and even if it were not wrong to think only of those things that touch ourselves we ought to see to these things being amended, for my goodman holds that if such things were not done in matters of this life, religion would not be so straitly directed and oppressed by the bishops as it now is. We have just heard ill news from our parson, which is the sorer trouble to Master Hampden, seeing he can do little to help the poor man."

"Why, what has happened now? another citation from the bishop?" asked Dame Saxby.

"Yes, it is even so. Some meddling body must have carried the news that the king's 'Book of Sports' has not been read in the church lately, but a godly and helpful sermon preached, wherein the duty of setting apart one day for God's service is enforced. Now, just as the winter is beginning, poor Master Drayton is summoned to appear in London, and we fear will be cast into prison there for his faithfulness; for he will not deny the charge brought against him, or promise to incite the people to foolish and often harmful mirth on the Lord's day."

"Dear heart! what is coming to our poor country? What will Master Drayton do?"

"What can he do but obey the bishop's call, and defend himself from the word of God?"

"I would not an I were he; I would not trust myself in the hands of any bishop, but would fly to the Low Countries, and join this expedition that is going to America. Master Cushman has great hopes that they may go next summer, for many helped him in raising the money needful."

"Master Hampden did suggest something of this, but our parson pleaded that he was getting to be an old man, and ill-fitted to encounter the dangers and hardships that will meet those who go out to form this new colony, and he fears to be a burden upon those who will have enough ado to shift for themselves."

"Well, well, there is something in that. But can Master Hampden do nothing for this godly minister? The bishop will, without doubt, dispossess him of this living; and I

know somewhat of this good man myself—
enough to make me anxious, Bessie."

"Yes, yes, we have seen you and Master
Saxby at church more than once, good dame,
and could not wonder that you left your own
parish church, where, I hear, there have been
many things to be seen in bowings and wearing fine cassocks, but little to be heard beyond the reading of the lessons and the king's
' Book of Sports.'"

"Ah, you have seen us here at Hampden,
Bessie; we hoped no one had noticed our
coming."

"We fear others have seen you as well as
ourselves," said young Dame Hampden, "and
my goodman was burning to give you a word
of warning."

"What mean you, my sweet Bess?" exclaimed Dame Saxby, now growing alarmed for
her own safety; for in those days heavy punishment often fell upon those who wandered
from their own parish church to another.

"Well, a notice has been sent from the
bishop warning all persons against the practice
of absenting themselves from their own parish
church; and so, as the eyes of those in authority are evidently turned toward our doings just
now, it is best to be circumspect."

"Yes, yes; I will take care not to offend in this way again, although it is hard to listen to the mouthings and mumblings which are all we get in our parish. Roger often laughs at our parson's ignorance and assumption of authority, and I often fear he is growing out of conceit of all religion through this very thing; but what can I do to mend matters?" and Dame Saxby sighed as she drew on her hood and prepared to take her departure. Her trouble about the silver lace was forgotten now in this fresh anxiety, and she hastened home to tell her husband all she had heard from young Dame Hampden.

5

CHAPTER V.

WAS IT WITCHCRAFT?

MASTER SAXBY did not appear to be
much surprised at what his wife told
him concerning the citation of Master Drayton.

"I've been expecting it," he said calmly.

"Expecting it! and yet you went to hear
him preach in another parish church!"

"Yes, and I shall go again an he preaches
again, for what right has the king or bishop
to command what I shall hear or believe?　It
is enough, I trow, that I cannot say what I
think of the ill doings and injustice of the
court and king without being robbed of my
liberty to serve God according to my own
conscience."

Dame Saxby looked at her husband, scarcely knowing what to think, for the calm determination of his tone astonished her; but still
she said, "Nay, but we must be cautious, and
go to our own church again."

"To listen to the reading of the 'Book of
Sports,' and see the popish mummings of our
parson?　A nice tale has come to my ears

concerning the doings of our Roger last Sunday; and when I spoke to him about it he said he was but obeying the king's command, and following the teaching of the parson and the king's 'Book of Sports;' and the lad was right."

"Nay, nay, but the 'Book of Sports' doth not enjoin drunkenness and brawling," said the dame quickly.

"Nay, but it sends the witless knaves into the midst of temptation, encouraging them in the drinking of ale more than is needful, and wrestling, and fencing, and dancing—all which often lead to brawling and worse. Had you heard of these ill doings, Moll?"

"Yes, I heard the wenches whispering among themselves, and I made Deb tell me; and then, by way of excusing the lad, she said, 'It was all because Harry had gone away.'"

"'Tis but a sorry way of showing his love for his brother. So Deb and the wenches were at the reveling?" said Master Saxby.

"Well, Deb said people began to whisper we were all Puritans and Precisians, and so I thought it better to let them go than bring that reproach upon ourselves."

"Puritans and Precisians, forsooth! My neighbors shall have liberty to call me that an they will, but I shall claim the liberty of ordering my family after a decent fashion, and not be bound a bond-slave to the king's ' Book of Sports.' "

" But — but you forget we have been to another parish church very often of late; twice on the Sunday, too," said Dame Saxby timidly. " It is against the law, I hear, that Master Drayton has preached on Sunday afternoons."

" Yes, yes, against the law, to be sure it is," said her husband impatiently; " but would you think about the law an a child were starving at your gates, and ye had bread to give him ?"

" Nay, nay; no one can say I ever turned a beggar hungry from my gate," said Dame Saxby; " I am free from that reproach."

" And Master Drayton would fain be the same—the only difference is, you have care for men's bodies and he for their souls, which are starving for lack of food."

" But what has that to do with preaching on Sunday afternoons?"

" Every thing, dame. Men were hungering for the bread of life, or they would not walk miles from other parishes to get it; and, seeing this, good Master Drayton provided them two meals instead of one. I wonder who the meddling body can be that has gone to the bishop with this tale about him."

It seemed that there must be some busy-bodies and mischief-makers among their own neighbors; for a little later, Deb, the cook, told her mistress that the blacksmith's wife had been talking to her about the strangers who had come to visit them a week or two before, and who had decoyed Master Harry to foreign parts, and how the village were all saying the Saxbies had turned Puritans, and forsaken their own parish church and the Sunday revels on the green.

"Nay, but, Deb, we never joined in these revels, or suffered the boys or serving-men to do so, until Roger took to going this summer."

"And little enough I care for the revels, where the boldest-faced minx is set above decent serving-wenches; but when they say you and my master are Puritans, and will not suffer us to join in their revels, it was time, I thought, to let them see we were no Puritans, although we did not go to their church ales and cakes."

Dame Saxby hardly knew what to say to this. Personally, she felt glad that Deb had adopted such an effectual means of warding off the charge of Puritanism being brought against them, and especially since it had be-

come known that they had been going of late
to another parish church; but whether her
husband would allow a continued attendance
at these festivities she did not know, but she
was resolved to do what she could to persuade
him to let Deb and the rest of the serving-
maids and men do as they liked in the matter.
They could shelter themselves under the plea
of being too old to join in such frolics, and
Roger and Larry must be warned to be more
circumspect in future.

But Master Saxby was by no means inclined
to yield to his wife in this. The thing was
wrong, he said. He was convinced that to
attend divine service in the morning and
spend the rest of the day in the ale-house, or
dancing and wrestling on the green, was little
better than a mockery, and he would have
nothing to do with it. On his wife venturing
to say that they would be accused of being
Puritans, he told her boldly that he had long
been a Puritan, and was no longer ashamed
of the name. Poor Dame Saxby was horror-
stricken to hear her husband speak out so
boldly, for she knew he would be likely to
avow it just as openly among the neighbors as
to herself, and she foresaw what trouble and
loss this would bring upon them. They might

even have to give up their rich farm lands—
be forced to sell them at a ruinous loss and
emigrate to Flanders or America—and she
shuddered at the thought of such a calamity
overtaking them, and the next minute burst
into tears.

" How now, dame, what ails you ? " asked
her husband, in some alarm ; for Dame Saxby
did not often shed tears.

" Can you ask me," she sobbed, " when you
talk of bringing us all to ruin ? If you only
cared—"

" Hush, hush, Moll, and let us talk this
matter over to ourselves. I ought to have
done it before, but I've been a coward even
with you ; but, God helping me, I mean to be
braver in future. I had a talk with Harry before he went away, God bless the lad ! and he
helped me to see things clearer as to what was
my duty in this matter. You'll see it too, I
trust, dame, and help me to do it."

" No one can ever say I haven't done my
duty," replied Dame Saxby quickly.

" That's true, dame, quite true ; you've been
a good wife, a good mother, and a good mistress. No one can say you haven't done your
duty to me and the boys; but I haven't done
mine, Moll."

"I should like to hear any body say that, and I would soon tell them what I thought about them," interrupted Dame Saxby.

"But I say it of myself, Moll. I have been a coward, ashamed to confess my Lord among men. I have not dared to own it even to you, but I tell you now, and I don't care who hears me say it, I am as much a Puritan as those who went away from here a few years ago, and I will go no more to the church in this parish to join in their half-Popish service. I tell you, Moll, the king is only half a Protestant; he has too strong a liking for his Popish mother's religion, and means to bring it back to us if he can—by degrees at first. Men's minds must be Romanized gradually through this half-Popish service. By and by a few more ceremonies will be added. After kneeling to take the sacrament the next step will be to adore the bread, as in the mass, and the table will be changed to an altar, and the communion called a sacrifice again. I talked with one or two in London, and this is the fear of many; and the only hope for England is in these Puritans she has been driving to other shores and other homes."

"Dear heart! what will happen next?" sighed poor Dame Saxby; "we shall be fined twelve pence for every Sunday we do not go to church, and you will be summoned before the bishop and made to promise that you will go to your own parish parson ; so that it will be better to go at once, without any trouble or setting our neighbors talking about us."

" Now, now, dame, this is not helping me," said her husband a little reproachfully.

" You want me to help you ruin yourself and the lads. What will Harry say, think you, when he hears the Saxby land has all been sold ? It is enough to make your father turn in his grave to think of it."

" But the Saxby land shall not be sold. It's been in the family for generations, and shall not go out of it in my time."

" You cannot help it if you turn Puritan ; great grandfather's curse will surely fall upon you, and the name of Saxby will cease to be known."

Master Saxby started as his wife brought this terrible curse to his memory. " What shall I do ? What can I do ? " he almost groaned. " I cannot live this lie any longer. The time has come when Master Hampden and I and one or two others must take a decided course one way or the other. We cannot abandon Master Drayton, who has been as an angel of

God to many of us; and to protect him will at
once bring upon us the notice of the bishop.
Perhaps we may all be summoned before the
Court of High Commission. There, you see,
dame, I have thought of what may happen—
what will very likely follow the course I mean
to pursue."

" And you are yet so obstinate, John Saxby,
that you will ruin your whole family and bring
down upon your head the curse that is sure to
follow upon the loss of the Saxby land?"
demanded his wife in mingled anger and astonishment.

"God help me! what am I to do, dame?
I never saw it to be my duty before as I do
now, but, seeing it as I do, I must do it. Yes,
I must!" he concluded.

" You will be summoned before the king at
Westminster, and fined and imprisoned. The
house and land will be sold to pay the fine,
and we shall be turned out with the family
curse for our portion, to beg our bread or
starve," said Dame Saxby.

" Hush, hush, dame; things shall not come
to that pass. I will go to-morrow and talk
with Master John Hampden. He knows a
little of the law, or he can find out from his
cousin, Master Oliver Cromwell, what I can do

to save the land. He is in London now, studying under some great lawyer, so that he may be the better landlord, as he has already lost his father. There, there, dame, no more tears. I will take care that Harry shall have the land, if the king and bishops have me for the rest of my days."

" It will be poor comfort to me to stay here and know you are in prison," sobbed his wife.

" It will keep my heart warm, though, to know the old homestead is sheltering you. But it is not so bad as that yet, dame, and, God helping us, it may not come to that."

" I believe you are bewitched as well as Master Hampden; and who can fight against witch spells? I mean to go out to-morrow and make inquiries as to whether any stranger has been seen lurking about here of late. It was only last week the brindled cow died, and Roger says several others seem ailing. What is all that but signs of witchcraft being abroad ? "

" O, but the cows are better now, Moll. The warm mash Hodge gave them this morning has done them good. I will go now and see that another is got ready for to-night, and to-morrow morning I will ride over to Hampden."

Dame Saxby turned away puzzled, angry,

and very anxious.   What could she do to avert
the evil that seemed likely to overwhelm them
with ruin ?   Her eldest, her darling, had been
taken away, she was certain, by the baleful
influence of witchcraft, and now her husband
seemed doomed, while she and her sons might
be reduced to beggary and shame.   Her husband might talk of God helping him to do his
duty, but if they had not always done their
duty she would like to know who had !   They
had gone to church regularly, either in their
own parish or at Hampden, paid all dues and
tithes, and helped the poor; and what more
could be expected of them she did not know.
This was the substance of Dame Saxby's self-
communing, as she stood at the window looking out upon the stubble fields and the fast-
falling leaves of the great beech-tree.

But idle self-communing was not long indulged by Dame Saxby.   She must go and
look after her maids, who, according to her
belief, were sure to be idling if her eye was
not upon them ; and if her husband was bent
upon wasting his money in fines she must try
and make it up a little by stricter economy in
the household.   Her thoughts thus set going
upon her usual household duties, eagerly on
the lookout for points where she might save a

few pence to help pay the weekly fines for not going to their own parish church, she spied in one corner a heap of dark-looking cloth, and, shaking it out, found it was a green baize table-cover, that Harry had had at Cambridge, but which had since been used to cover a small table in Roger's room. It was almost an unheard-of luxury; but Dame Saxby thought to please her son by giving him this memento of Harry's Cambridge life when he went away, and therefore to see it thrown here, as if of no value, vexed her not a little. But as she shook it out she saw that it was stained with spots of oil, as though a lamp had been shaken or upset over it; and, vexed beyond expression at such waste, she went with it at once to Deb, who, being the oldest of her "wenches," was usually favored with most of her confidences and most of her scoldings. As a matter of course Deb was scolded for the damaged table-cover, and when her angry mistress had said all she could think of concerning the idleness, carelessness, and extravagance of serving-wenches, Deb quietly told her all she knew about the matter. Mistress and maid knew each other thoroughly, and if there was a quiet tone of calm disdain underlying the respectful words used by the

cook, Dame Saxby took no notice of it. She
had relieved her feelings by scolding Deb, and
now she was ready to hear any thing that
could be said in explanation of what had happened. But she was scarcely prepared to hear
what Deb had to tell—that Roger had never
liked the table-cover being in his room, and
had told Deb to take it away or he should
throw it away. The oil had been spilt by ac-
cident, she believed. Roger told her he had
upset the lamp after he came home from the
wake on Sunday, but she did not know that
the table-cover had been spoiled, or that it
had been brought down stairs.

" But it is spoiled; I can never use it for a
table-cover again. Such shameful, willful waste.
What am I to do with it?" demanded the angry lady, holding it out again to look at it.

"It would make a good warm pair of winter
stockings for Roger," said Deb.

" So it would. I never thought of that,
Deb. The master has brought some cloth
from London, and I thought to cut a pair of
stockings from that, but Roger's shall be cut
from this instead. It would serve him right
to cut them with the grease spots in; but we
need not do that. Still, Master Roger shall
remember despising his brother's things."

CHAPTER VI.

IN LONDON.

THE result of Master Saxby's conference with his neighbor, Master John Hampden, made him decide to pay another visit to London; but his object in going there he kept a secret even from his wife at present, to her great annoyance and indignation.

Dame Saxby, however, had a secret of her own, which she was very anxious her husband should not discover just yet at least. By and by she might want his assistance to bring the witch-wife to justice; but at present she had little more than her own prejudice and a little village gossip to convict the poor old woman, who, up to the present time, had always borne a good character among her neighbors. But there certainly had been some mysterious proceedings of late. A tall stranger, shrouded in a long cloak, and wearing a slouched hat, had been seen to leave her cottage after night-fall more than once lately. The blacksmith's wife declared she had seen the shape of a tail under the cloak, and another thought there was a

faint smell of sulphur in the lane after he had
passed ; but, worse than all these surmises,
there remained the actual fact that there was
a great deal of sickness among the cattle just
now, which, according to the belief of those
times, could only be accounted for by witchcraft.   So Dame Saxby's vague hints that she
knew there was a witch somewhere in the
neighborhood found only too ready credence
among the gossips of the place, and there were
plenty ready to watch old Gammer Grove, and
bring the mistress news of all they might discover.

Dame Saxby went home well satisfied with
the result of her inquiries, and only anxious
lest her husband should spoil the whole plot
by some premature step which would warn the
old woman that she was watched.   She took
care to be home before her husband could be
back from Hampden, lest he should inquire
where she had been.   But she need not have
hurried herself.   Master. Saxby did not get
back until supper-time, and then he was so
grave and preoccupied that he did not notice
even the absence of Roger, who had gone out
early in the afternoon, and had not yet returned.

When Larry heard that his father was going

to London he begged that he might go with him, but Master Saxby declared he must go alone; his errand was important, and he should have no time to take him to see the sights and amusements of the place. So the long-talked-of visit must be deferred until the spring.

When Dame Saxby found that this important errand was to be kept a secret even from her she grumbled a little; but then told her husband he need not be at so much pains to keep this a secret when all the village would know within a week that he had gone on business concerning Master Drayton's appearing before the bishop.

Her husband did not contradict this assertion, and Dame Saxby went on: "I suppose you and John Hampden have decided to stand by Master Drayton and defy the bishop, and the king himself if need be."

"Well, we had a long talk about the good man, and we both hold that it is our duty to help him. Master Hampden says if he had children to instruct he would take him into his house as chaplain, but, that not being so, he is willing to devote a certain sum to his maintenance as a lecturer; by which means Hampden will profit by his godly teaching still, and he hopes that some others in the neighboring villages will also contribute something as well."

"Of course you promised to do so, in spite of the risk and the fines you will have to pay," said Dame Saxby crossly.

"I could not do less, Moll, seeing what a debt I owe to Master Drayton."

"Well, I hope doing this will satisfy you, then, and that you will go to your own church without any more trouble coming upon us."

Master Saxby shook his head; but his wife, thinking she had found the clew of this obstinacy, and would soon be able to deprive the witch of her power over him, let the matter drop, convinced that things would soon work round into their usual state again when Gammer Grove was got rid of.

Master Saxby set out on his journey alone, but was glad to join a party of travelers for safety's sake before they reached London; for the neighborhood of Hounslow and Hampstead was infested with robbers, and it was only by traveling in large parties, and all well armed, that the traveler could hope to reach his destination in safety.

By the time the city was reached his horse was well-nigh worn out with his two days'

journey and the speed to which he had been
urged the last few miles. Never had the low-
ing of his own cattle been more welcome to Master Saxby's ears than the cries of the city apprentices as they plied their masters' trade.

"What do you lack? What do you lack?
Buy a watch or a horologe?" cried one.
"What do you lack? A silken girdle or a
velvet cloak, a satin doublet or woven hose?
Walk in, my masters, walk in and choose the
best in London town," shouted a pushing
mercer's lad, hustling the passengers and plac-
ing himself right in Master Saxby's way.

"Nay, nay, my good lad, I want not silken
hose or satin doublet, but a decent hostelry
where I can refresh myself and my tired
horse." Master Saxby had alighted, and was
leading the poor jaded animal, which had
fallen lame. This consideration of the country
farmer seemed to touch the London apprentice, and, darting into the crowd after a fair-
haired school-boy about ten or eleven years
old, who had just passed, he called, "Johnny,
John Milton, here, take this stranger to the
'Mermaid!' 'Tis a decent hostelry, sir, in
Broad-street, and right opposite Master Milton's, the scrivener," said the apprentice, turning to Master Saxby.

“ Is your father the scrivener, my little lad ? ” asked Master Saxby, as the gentle-looking, fair-haired boy placed himself at his side.

“ Yes, sir ; we live at the sign of the ‘ Spread Eagle,’ in Broad-street, and the ‘ Mermaid,’ where, my father says, Master Will Shakspeare and Ben Jonson and other poets used to meet a year or two ago, is a little farther down, not quite opposite, as Tom Simmons said.”

“ Is Tom Simmons your friend, my lad ? ”

“ N-no, not such a friend as Gill, my schoolmaster’s son.　Gill can write poetry.”

“ And would you like to write poetry ? ” asked Master Saxby, looking down into the fair, refined face of the little boy.

“ Yes, sir ; it is almost as good as music, I think, and my father writes music, you know.”

“ Does he ?　But I thought you said he was a scrivener—at least that lad did.”

“ Yes, he is.　But you must not always believe what Tom Simmons says.　He told a lie once, and said he had been with me to Allhallows Church to hear godly Master Gataker, but he told me he would not come to hear that Puritan, and went to Holborn Fields to gather May boughs.”

" Is the minister at Allhallows a Puritan, my little lad ?"

" Yes, sir, I think so. My father says he preaches godly sermons, although he will not have us follow the king's ' Book of Sports.' "

" Then is your father a Puritan too ? " asked Master Saxby rather eagerly.

" I suppose so. Master Stocke, the parson of Allhallows, and Master Gataker, of Rotherhithe, often come to see my father, and Tom Simmons says they are both Puritans."

" Ah, ah ! then I think I shall come home with you, my lad, and ask your father to do some scrivener's work for me," said Master Saxby with something of a sigh of relief, for he had been wondering who he could get to execute the work he wanted done. This secret of his was a weighty one, and it would not do to intrust it to any body ; but if this Master Milton was a godly man and a Puritan he would be able to understand the need there was for this work being done promptly and thoroughly.

They had turned out of the bustle and din of Cheapside now into the more quiet Broadstreet, and a few minutes brought them to the scrivener's door. The boy darted in at once and Master Saxby soon followed to where a grave, elderly man sat writing at a desk, with two or three apprentices close by.

Master John Milton laid down his pen and pushed the parchment on one side to listen to his little son's tale of the stranger he had brought home with him; but when Master Saxby came forward himself the child left them and went into the room at the back of the shop to tell his mother and sister of his adventure.

Master Saxby was certainly prepossessed by the grave sweetness of the old scrivener's face; but still he needed to be cautious, and so, merely saying he had some weighty work to be executed, if Master Milton thought he could use dispatch, and promising to call again when the scrivener was less busy, he asked a few questions about the " Mermaid " as a hostelry, and what sort of a parson they had in this parish, which led Master Milton to invite the stranger to call upon him that evening, when the shop was closed, as he expected the minister and his worthy friend, Master Gataker, to call upon him.

This Master Saxby readily promised to do, for it would give him time to follow his friend Hampden's advice, and he would walk up·to Gray's Inn as soon as he had his dinner, and find out Oliver Cromwell, to consult him about the best scrivener to be employed upon his business. Perhaps he might know this Master Milton, or could find out whether he was a man to be trusted in this delicate affair. Having settled this matter in his own mind he felt at liberty to rest and refresh himself when he had seen that his horse was well cared for.

Dinner over, Master Saxby set out on his walk to Gray's Inn, near Holborn fields; but catching sight of Master Milton's face as he passed his shop, he almost decided to intrust the business to him, whether Oliver Cromwell knew him or not, so anxious did he feel to make his acquaintance and see more of the child, who reminded him so much of his own dear Harry. After all, Oliver was little more than a lad himself, and would, perhaps, have few opportunities of knowing what these scriveners were, although a good deal of their work would, doubtless, pass throngh his hands in the course of his law studies.

He had little trouble in finding the young student, and had soon told him the business that brought him to London, and also his meeting with little John Milton, on his way home from St. Paul's school.

But young Cromwell knew nothing of Master Milton, although he knew a certain city knight, Sir James Bouchier, who probably did know him, and, with the greatest alacrity, he proposed taking his cousin's friend with him at once to consult the wealthy furrier upon the matter in hand. Master Saxby demurred at giving so much trouble, but young Cromwell declared he thought little of the trouble, and as he was engaged to sup with the knight's family it would be of little consequence that he went an hour earlier.

Arrived at the wealthy city merchant's house, it was easy to see that Master Oliver was welcome, whatever the business might be that brought him, especially to Mistress Elizabeth, the eldest of the merchant's daughters ; and Master Saxby noted it as a piece of gossip to be taken home to his wife.

As young Cromwell had surmised, Sir James did know something of Master Milton ; had heard him spoken of as the most trusty scrivener in London, and one to whom he would himself confide any business of weight and secrecy without hesitation.

But he would not hear of his visitor returning to the " Mermaid " until he had supped, although Master Saxby declared he was not fit to sit down with ladies, as he had not

brought a change of dress with him. But the
merchant laughed off these scruples, and kept
him talking so long about crops and cattle,
and the prospects of the country, that it was
five o'clock and supper-time before he was
aware of it.

Those were not the days when culinary
matters were left to a servant entirely, and
the merchant's daughters prided themselves
on being able to set a well-cooked meal on
their father's table ; and doubtless Mistress
Elizabeth had taken extra pains with the
salads to-day in anticipation of the visit of
Oliver Cromwell. There were boar's head
and venison pasties, boiled salmon from the
Thames, and calves' foot pies; but the most
intricate and delicate dishes to prepare were
the vegetables, or salads, as they were then
called. A dish of boiled mashed carrots, to
which was added cinnamon, sugar, ginger, a
handful of currants, vinegar, and butter, was
considered very rich, while one of marigold
leaves, with similar additions, was considered
very choice.

Master Saxby was inclined to turn up his
nose at this fine cooking ; but it was evident
that young Cromwell was ready to be pleased
with any thing that Mistress Elizabeth had

done, and praised the housewifely care be-
stowed on the preparation of these dishes.

When supper was over, and the table cleared
away, the young people prepared to amuse
themselves with singing, and Master Saxby
had a little further talk with Sir James Bouchier, during which it came out that he was
as stanch a Puritan as the Cromwells, and
would not suffer young Oliver to visit them
as he did if he were not assured that he was
a steady, God-fearing young man, earnestly
striving to fit himself for the responsible duties
devolving upon him as an elder son, who must,
to a certain extent, take upon himself the duties of his father toward his sisters and mother,
and the neighborhood in which he lived.

"He has told me it was no easy matter for
him to give up the quiet pursuit of learning
at Cambridge, when his father died, to come
up here and learn something of the practice
of the law; but he saw that if ever he was to
make a wise and just landlord, and—as he
probably will be some day—a justice·of the
peace to his neighbors, he must know something of this matter. So he has resolutely set
himself to do his duty, regardless of what his
wishes may be; and may God bless and honor
him for it!" said the knight warmly.

"Ah, ah, to do one's duty is not always the easiest thing in the world," said Master Saxby, with something of a sigh.

"Nay, nay; and our young men often think that they have little to do but enjoy themselves—running off to practice archery at the Butts, by Southwark or in Moorfields, thinking little of their master's business, and less about the duty they owe to them."

This was said for the benefit of two 'prentice lads, who were standing near, waiting to speak to their master before he left the shop again.

It was quite dark by this time, and so Sir James, turning to these two, bade them get a link and light Master Saxby through the city to Broad-street, and having seen him safe to the "Spread Eagle," to return without delay and help count the skins that had just been delivered.

CHAPTER VII.

A SOCIAL EVENING.

MASTER SAXBY was not sorry to reach his destination in Broad-street, and very thankful to the lads who had conducted him in safety through the dark, narrow, ill-kept streets; for there was not only the danger of falling in some of the numerous ruts and holes with which these abounded, but robberies with violence were of frequent occurrence after night-fall, even in the very heart of the city, and in spite of the watch that patrolled its streets for the protection of wayfarers. The fact was, the cunning thieves knew the time when the watchmen might be expected in a certain quarter, and even if the cries of their victim brought the welcome, " Ho, ho," from the watch, or brought a few citizens from their houses, the darkness made their capture almost impossible, if they were at all dexterous; and so it came to pass that few, beyond those whom dire necessity compelled, ever went out after nightfall, unless it was to visit a neighbor a few steps from their own door, and they could go and return while the watch were close by to protect them. The two 'prentice lads who had conducted him through the streets carried each a stout stick, and assured him several times there was no danger; for if any one attacked them, they would soon raise the cry of "Clubs, clubs!" which would bring forth from the houses all the free "'prentices" of London, and Master Saxby knew enough of "'prentice" customs to know that the boast was by no means a vain one; but still he was thankful to reach Master Milton's door without such an adventure.

The two ministers, Master Stocke and Master Gataker, had already arrived, the children had gone to bed, and placid Dame Milton sat sewing some cloth hose for her little John. She was some years younger than her husband, whom she looked up to with a reverence that made itself apparent even to Master Saxby, while the old scrivener evidently regarded her as a companion to be most tenderly cherished and loved.

Room was made for the stranger-guests at once in the pleasant family circle, and news from the country, especially as regarded Puritanism, was eagerly asked for, and the troubles of poor Master Drayton were at once told, and almost before he was aware of it he had told his present errand to London.

He was afraid the share he was about to take in the protecting and helping Master Drayton would lead to ruinous fines being imposed upon him, which would eventually lead to the loss of his patrimony, which he was most anxious his son should inherit intact. So, by the advice of his neighbor, Master John Hampden, he had come to London to get the necessary deeds executed, giving this to his eldest son at once, and constituting himself, and, in case of his death or inability to fulfill the duties, his second son Roger, trustees until Harry should return and claim the gift. In case of Harry's death he wished it to be provided that the estate should go to his children, or, in case of his dying childless, to revert to Roger or Lawrence. The secret fear concerning his great-grandfather's curse falling upon his children he kept to himself; but still it was a powerful factor in actuating him to take all these precautions against the land passing away from the Saxby family.

"Then it is still dangerous to profess a pure doctrine, or to strive for purity of worship," said Master Stocke, the minister of Allhallows. The London ministers were at this time less

open to persecution than many of their brethren, for the Bishop of London and the Archbishop of Canterbury had a strong leaning
toward Puritanism themselves, and so were
not likely to search for it very rigorously, as
many other bishops did. In addition to this,
and a more powerful reason, the citizens were
almost entirely Puritan in their principles, and
they were too useful in granting subsidies and
benevolences to the needy monarch to be offended with impunity in the matter of their
religious convictions.

"We are in less evil case than our brethren
of the country," said Master Gataker; "for,
though we cannot hope for much in the way
of preferment to high places in the Church,
many things imposed upon our brethren are
not forced upon us."

"But you are compelled to read the king's
'Book of Sports,' exhorting the people to
break the Sabbath," said Master Saxby.

"The king commanded us so to do, but
when the king's command is contrary to the
teaching of God's word, think you any godly
minister would hesitate whom he should obey?
'Tis but few pulpits in London where the
'Book of Sports' is read," concluded Master
Gataker.

"Ah, but in our parish they preach the doctrine that it is a man's duty to obey the king above all things ; that his right to rule is divine, and even in matters of conscience it is treason to disobey him."

The old Puritan divine shook his head gravely. "The sin of treason is as the sin of witchcraft, and no man dare counsel that any should commit that. But, then, although kings be the ministers appointed by God to rule over us, I hold not that our King James is but another pope to order the things pertaining to the Church according to his will. An he rule us according to God's law we are bound to obey him, as saith St. Paul, 'Fear God, honor the king.'"

"Ah, ah, but in this time-serving age too many of our parsons forget St. Paul, or reverse the order of his command. It has grown fashionable, specially in our parts, to preach much about obeying the king, but little about the fear of God," said Master Saxby.

"Yes, yes, we have heard of it, and of the tribulation of many of our brethren, who have dared to declare the whole counsel of God in this matter, and we know not what to do, or what this thing will grow to by and by. We

who love the doctrine of Calvin, and would
fain see our Church more like that of Geneva
in its freedom from Romish practices — we
would rather also see the king more favorable
to his Scottish subjects in their love of Presbyterianism than so anxious to force bishops
and a prayer-book upon them."

" Nay, but the king has taken the greatest
care to uphold the doctrine of Calvin by the
deputies sent to take part in the disputation
with Arminius at Dort," said Master Milton,
quickly.

" Yes, yes, he will oppose Arminius to his
face, and force the Dutch to a persecution of
him if he can ; and yet it is feared by many
that his dislike of Presbyterianism, which gives
men higher thoughts of civil liberty, arises
from his overweening love of kingly authority,
which may yet lead him covertly to favor Arminianism as a spiritual power to uphold his
kingly right in all things."

But Master Milton did not hold this rather
gloomy view of the old Puritan divine. Things
were bad enough, he knew, but he hoped the
next change might be for the better. The
power of the House of Commons was certainly
on the increase. The spread of learning all over the country had raised the intelli-

7

gence of the people, and the king could not control the election of members, as once had been the custom.

"King James hardly understood this when he told the Parliament a few years ago 'that as it was blasphemy to question what the Almighty could do by his power, so it was sedition to inquire what a king could do by virtue of his prerogative.'"

"Ah, ah, that was a bold speech, and made many tremble, I trow," remarked Master Saxby.

"Doubtless many trembled; but not our brave Commons; for not long afterward they boldly told the king that 'new laws could not be instituted, nor imperfect laws reformed, nor inconvenient laws abrogated by any other power than that of the high court of Parliament;' that is, by the agreement of the Commons, the accord of the Lords, and the assent of the king," said Master Milton, triumphantly.

"Yes, yes, the struggle has begun, but when and how will it end?" said Master Gataker, with something of a sigh.

"The king has certainly put an end to this struggle for the present by ruling without a Parliament, and I have heard that their boast-

ed power could not save one Master Pym
from imprisonment for vaunting words spoken
in this same Parliament," remarked Master
Saxby.

" That is true enough," assented Master
Milton ; " but there are already whispers
abroad that the king will be compelled to call
another Parliament ere long, and men are preparing themselves for the struggle, for many
things need reforming in the State as well as
in the Church."

" An the king will let us worship God according to our own conscience, would it not
be better to leave other things alone and not
meddle with the king's prerogative ? " questioned gentle Dame Milton.

But her husband shook his head, and Master Stocke remarked, " The Reformation has
taught men to think for themselves, to inquire
into the use and value of many things our fathers reverenced without understanding them.
The uselessness and evil of many of these led
them to overthrow the religious tyranny by
which they had been governed for centuries,
and now the secular power must reform at the
bidding of this same principle, or it will share
the fate of the Church that governed England
before the Reformation."

"They are bold words, my brother," said the elder divine, warningly.

"It were better for Christians to let the world alone, I trow," said Dame Milton.

"Nay, nay, dame; that might be an our blessed Saviour had never said, 'Ye are the salt of the earth,'" said her husband, tenderly, patting the smooth white hand that had been laid upon his shoulder as if to stay him in this dangerous work they were discussing.

"Ah, dame, 'tis a pity the world cannot be reformed without all this struggling and fighting," remarked Master Saxby with a sigh, as he thought of his son and the struggle going on in the Protestant States of Germany.

"I have so often thought of Master Pym being shut up in the Gate-house when the Parliament was over, and of Dame Pym and her bitter disappointment and anxiety when he did not reach home as she expected, and all this suffering for a few brave words that did but anger the king—"

"Nay, nay, dame; Master Pym did but speak the thoughts of many in England to-day, and 'tis but fair to warn the king that we will not wear the yoke he would fain impose upon us."

"But 'tis all about worldly matters the Parliament concerns itself," objected the lady; "if it were a matter of conscience, such as you have suffered for, John, I would not say one word against it."

John Milton had come of a noble, wealthy, Catholic family, and his friends had cast him off on his embracing the Protestant faith. It was to this his wife referred.

" Nay, but dame, State matters and Church matters—the right to worship God after our own hearts' desire—are so interwoven now that we cannot separate them. Spiritual and civil liberty are bound up together, and both must be won or lost in this struggle," said Master Stocke.

" I cannot bear to think of it," said the lady with a shiver of apprehension. It was but yesterday I heard of another man being seized for speaking against the Court of Star-chamber, and none. can tell who may be the next even for speaking against these shameful new monopolies."

" That is true enough, dame. But think you honest folk ought quietly to give up their money to enrich such creatures as this Sir Giles Mompesson and the court gallant Buckingham, without a lawful protest being made against this most unlawful exaction ? "

"But who would dare to make the protest?" asked Dame Milton.

"None would have the right to do it but Parliament, and they will doubtless tell the king that this thing may not be repeated except by their consent."

"And then some more good, brave men will be thrust into prison, and their wives and little children be plunged into sorrow and mourning. Nay, nay, I would rather pay ten times as much for my currants, and never more wear silver lace than that this should happen."

"Ah, dame, I can feel for you there," said Master Gataker; "but, I fear me, if the same spirit was in our Parliament men we should have to leave out in our readings those precious words of David: 'The earth is the Lord's, and the fullness thereof,' for it would be full of violence and extortion, and the devil would soon have it all his own way. Nay, nay, the world belongs to God still, and we wont give it up to the devil, hard as he may try for it."

"But think of the sorrow and the suffering! Only last week I saw a man in the pillory for writing something that had given offense to the king and council."

"Ah, true, dame; and there was a cross reared once on a green hill-top, and one suf-

fered there more cruel pangs than those of the
pillory; and all because he so loved the world
that he would not let the devil keep the prize
he thought he had cheated God of. He never
taught us that God's work of saving the world
could be easily or cheaply done, and so we
must not be surprised at the struggling and
fighting, or shrink from bearing our part in it,
if God call us to endure it. Now, friends, let
us pray. This is the true source of strength
and courage and all might;" and Master Gataker prayed with a fervor that carried all hearts
with him, and made even timid Dame Milton
forget her fears for the present.

Then the Bible was brought out, and Master
Gataker turned its leaves over to the account
of Gideon, and his heroic deeds on behalf of
an oppressed people; and read it aloud in such
tones of thrilling power that every heart was
stirred and strengthened, and almost longed
for some call of duty bidding them emulate
the noble deeds of the heroic old Hebrew.

Whatever we may think, and whatever critics
may say, about this portion of God's word, it
is incontestible that our Puritan forefathers—
the heroes of their own and of every age—
drew inspiration, strength, and courage by
drawing deeply and largely from this well of

salvation.　Many a weak heart, wearied with the long, long struggle of right against might, came back to this old story of Gideon, and read, with ever-rising courage and hope, the glorious triumphant song of Deborah and Barak.　Even their very weakness was turned into a source of strength, and was gloried in and triumphed over, as making them the chosen instruments of God to confound the wise and mighty of the world.　We read the same soul-stirring words now, and our hearts break into a song, but little do we know of their sweetness and strength as compared with those held perhaps within prison walls for essaying to do some noble deed, or uttering some true brave words, yet comforting themselves with the thought that the battle was no uncertain one, since God was on their side; and though they might be shut up and never permitted to lift a hand again in the fight, others would grasp the standard and press on to victory.

Some such thoughts as these rested in the hearts of all our friends as they separated for the night.　They could hear the watch approaching, and under their escort Master Saxby would return to the "Mermaid," and the ministers would go together to the home of Master Stocke, close to All-hallows Church.

CHAPTER VIII.

GAMMER GROVE.

MASTER SAXBY'S stay in London was not a long one, but while the necessary deeds were being prepared he contrived to see little John Milton very often, and most of his evenings were spent in the quiet family circle listening to the music of which Master Milton was so fond, or talking to gentle Dame Milton as she sat sewing. But the week in London soon came to an end, and with a promise to call and see the scrivener whenever he should visit the great city again, Master Saxby once more turned his steps homewards. He went a mile or two out of his way to call upon John Hampden and leave the deeds for him to look over, and there he was met with a tale of fresh troubles having fallen upon Master Drayton.

"Some meddlesome body in Great Kimble has accused poor old Gammer Grove of being a witch, because they saw Master Drayton leave her cottage after dark. It was not deemed safe that the ministers who have met together with him for the study of God's Word should go to his house just now, since the place is doubtless watched by the bishop's spies, and so Gammer Grove's cottage was chosen as the place of meeting — Master Drayton knowing her to be a godly, steadfast woman, not likely to betray them. Little did he think it could bring trouble upon her, seeing she was held in such high esteem by the neighbors. But a day or two ago, when she went through the village, a few of the idle lads set up the cry after her, 'a witch! a witch!' and yesterday, when she went to inquire after the blacksmith's sick child, the door was slammed in her face, and she was accused of making the little fellow ill, as well as causing all the sickness among the cattle in the neighborhood. Then another angry woman asked her who the tall stranger was, with horns and hoofs, who came to visit her so often; which at once convinced the poor old woman what was the cause of the accusation. She begged Master Drayton not to come again to her cottage, and she hoped the affair would blow over; but he is anxious to go at once and declare the whole business, and I hardly know what to advise in the matter."

" Leave it to me, Master Hampden, and tell Master Drayton not to stir in the business, and I'll protect poor old Gammer Grove, never fear," said Master Saxby, quickly. "The witless knaves must surely be mad to accuse that poor old woman of being a witch. Why, she was always ready to lend a helping hand to any one in trouble, and when there was so much sickness in the village two years ago, Gammer Grove was nurse to every poor body in turn."

"Well, well, if you can make them see reason, neighbor Saxby, I shall be glad if Master Drayton can be spared making any stir in the matter, as it might bring trouble to two or three other ministers in these parts; but remember the poor old woman must be protected at all costs," said Master Hampden.

"Never fear, never fear but I will protect her," said the farmer, rising as he spoke.

The deeds had been handed to Master Hampden, and a few words said about the worthy scrivener who had drawn them up; and had there been time more would have been said about the meeting with the two Puritan divines at Master Milton's house, but Master Saxby was anxious to reach home now, with as little delay as possible. He, therefore, urged his horse to a brisk canter as soon as he left Master Hampden's door. At first he thought he would stop at the blacksmith's shed, and inquire what the village news was, and whether any thing had happened during his absence, as he frequently did when he had been a few days from home, but second thoughts made him decide to go straight home and get the news there. His dame would be sure to have heard all the village gossip, and ready enough to tell him every thing that had happened, which the blacksmith might not be very forward to do if he had joined in this foolish outcry against poor old Gammer Grove.

So he did not draw rein until he reached the porch before his own door, where his wife appeared the next minute to meet and welcome him home.

As soon as the first greetings were over and Hodge had been called to take his horse to the stable, Master Saxby said quickly, "What is all this about Gammer Grove, Moll?"

"Gammer Grove?" repeated the dame, bustling off to prepare a meal for her hungry husband. "Here, Deb, bring that cold chine, and Sally come and set the table ready for supper," she called, as she hurried to the dairy to get some fresh butter.

Master Saxby saw it would be little use questioning his wife until supper was on the table, at least, but Roger and Larry coming in at that moment, he at once began questioning them. Lawrence did not answer his father's question at all, but left his elder brother to do this, while he went and stood at the window.

Roger hesitated, and seemed confused when his father said, " My lad, I want you tell me all you know about this foolish business of Gammer Grove being a witch."

" But I don't know that it is so foolish, father," said Roger, plucking up a little courage at last. " There's a witch about somewhere, that's certain, and more than one person in these parts is bewitched, to say nothing of the cattle that's dying all round. Our Cowslip's dead."

" Cowslip ? " repeated the farmer ; " how came you to let that happen ? I wouldn't have spared fifty pounds to save that cow."

" We did all we could, father. Hodge sat up all the night before last to see that the witch did not come nigh the barn, and he used all sorts of things to break the spells, but it was all of no use ; there's no fighting against witch spells ; and they say Gammer Grove is a bad one, for all she is so demure."

" Gammer Grove a witch ! Why you will say your own mother is one next, you witless knave," said Master Saxby, half angrily.

" But there's Cowslip, and she's not the only cow that's died about here lately," objected Roger.

" Poor Cowslip! I wish I had been home before she died. But still, I'll never believe Gammer Grove had any thing to do with her sickness or death. There must be some disease among the cattle just now. A kind-hearted old woman like the gammer, who has nursed every child in the village and been ready to do any body a good turn, would never kill my cows."

" Not until the devil got hold of her," said Roger—a sentiment he devoutly believed in himself.

But Master Saxby shook his head. " I doubt whether the devil comes so readily unless he is invited, and we know Gammer Grove too well to think that of her. Besides, Roger, I know the gammer has had nothing to do with this business," concluded Master Saxby in a decided tone.

" Well, father, I might have said the same about the gammer once, but it's no use going against the whole village when they've seen the Evil One leaving her cottage more than once—ay, and smelt him too," concluded Roger.

" What will the witless knaves say next ? " exclaimed Master Saxby.

" It 's true enough, I can tell you, father."

" That they said it ? Well, perhaps so ; but what will you say, Roger, when I tell you that I know who it was left Gammer Grove's cottage, and that he was an honest gentleman who little thought to get the poor old woman into trouble through it ? "

But Roger was still unconvinced. All the village said she was a witch, and how could his father know any thing about it, since he had been in London ever since the discovery had been made ? At this moment Dame Saxby came in, and her husband at once turned to question her.

" Don't ask me what I think about the deceitful, wicked old woman, to kill my favorite cow because she saw I was finding out her wickedness and how she was bewitching every body and making every thing miserable for us."

" Come, come, dame, I shall think you are bewitched if you talk like this of poor old Gammer Grove," said her husband.

" Well, perhaps I am. At all events some folks not far from me are ! " snapped the dame.

" Perhaps we are all bewitched together,"

said Roger, in a grumbling tone, glancing down at the stockings that had been made for him out of his brother's table cover. Every private grievance that any body had against another was being set down to the spells Gammer Grove had woven against them; and as Harry, in his kindly good nature, had often spoken a pleasant word, or helped the old woman home with a load of sticks, Roger had taken up the notion that it was through the spells of witchcraft he was such a favorite with his mother and every body who knew him, and that she had worked against him to a like degree. What but this ill feeling against him could have made his mother cut his stockings out of the damaged table-cover that had been Harry's? Not that there was any fault specially to be found with the stockings; they were as good as—perhaps rather better than—those he usually wore, and Larry had a pair like them, but then Larry's had been cut from cloth specially provided, and not from his brother's left-off things; and here lay the sting to Roger. Of course he dared not give vent to these feelings aloud, but he nursed them in his own heart, and they grew in bitterness, day by day, increasing the dislike, almost hatred, he felt against his absent brother, and often

making him morose and gloomy even toward
Larry.

Master Saxby knew not what to do when
he heard his wife declare her belief in the
charge brought against poor old Gammer Grove.
He was both surprised and disappointed too,
for he had secretly relied upon receiving both
help and advice from his shrewd wife in this
delicate affair; and to find himself thus suddenly thrown upon his resources was a puzzle
he knew not how to solve.

He had no appetite for supper now, and
even the savory pie that had been specially
prepared for his home-coming was pushed
aside almost untasted, to Dame Saxby's great
vexation, who began to fear now that her husband was going to be ill, since he could not
eat savory pie.

In vain the poor man protested that he was
only tired from his long journey, and a little
put out by this business of Gammer Grove's.
His wife would not believe in the one, and declared that the old woman was not worth
troubling about, and the sooner she was out of
the way the better.

Master Saxby did not attach much importance to these last words, and soon after the
table was cleared away he went to bed to try

8

and think out some plan of action for the next day, for something must be done at once to stop the general outcry against the poor old woman, or there was no telling how it might end.

Meanwhile Dame Saxby and Roger were talking over the same matter down-stairs, and if the farmer could only have heard the conference he would probably have got up that very night and sought further aid on the poor old woman's behalf.

"What do you think now, my son, about your father and this witch-wife?" said Dame Saxby, when she and Roger were left to themselves.

Roger shrugged his shoulders. "I don't know what to think. My father says he knows who it is that has been to her cottage of late."

"Of course he says so; of course the old witch has made her tale good—told him it was some Puritan parson, I dare say; for, now I come to think of it, she used to be reckoned a Puritan when there was such a rout among them, ten or twelve years ago; and though I never heard any of them accused of witchcraft, depend upon it they don't mind seeking its aid to get the help and countenance of a rich man like your father. It 's through her witch spells that she has made him so ready to lose every thing for the sake of declaring himself a Puritan."

Dame Saxby had talked herself out of breath in her anger, and now paused. "But how are we to stop the mischief now, mother?" said Roger. "I cannot bear to see my father ruin himself, as he will do, I am sure; for only to-day, when I met Parson Crane, he stopped and asked me if it was true that my father had determined to protect that treasonable Puritan in the next parish."

"What did you tell him, Roger?" asked Dame Saxby. "It will not do to offend Master Crane now, you know," she added.

"I said I knew little of my father's affairs, but that I always meant to abide by my own parish church, and never run after sectaries, whoever they might be."

"That's right, Roger; and we must all be careful to be seen in our places at church, too. To-morrow you shall carry Master Crane a couple of fowls and a score of eggs. If he cannot preach a sermon he has the ear of the bishop, I'm told, and may make things lighter for your father, if the worst comes to the worst. And, now, about this witch; she must be got rid of somehow. I wish she would go right away from the place, and never come back."

"What would be the good of that, if she left her spells upon my father and—and the rest of us?" asked Roger, significantly. "No, mother, we must try her in the usual way, and the sooner the better. Some of them were talking about it yesterday; the pond is pretty full now, and—"

"But I should not like her to be drowned, Roger. She saved poor Harry's life when he was struck with the plague, and I was worn out with nursing him; for no one else would come nigh the house."

"Well, mother, every body has got some such tale about the old woman, and yet you were the first to get up this cry against her. What is it you do want?"

Truth to tell, the fact of having saved his brother's life, and so prevented him from inheriting the rich Saxby lands, did not tell much in the old woman's favor with Roger, and he rather angrily repeated, "Now, mother, tell us what it is you do want."·

"Well, Roger, I shouldn't like to think the poor old woman was drowned, and through me, too; but if you could threaten her with it, and drive her away from the village, so that she'd be afraid ever to show her head in these parts again, things would soon come right of themselves, I know."

"Well, mother, we'll try your plan if we can, though I don't see much difference myself in drowning the old witch outright and driving her away to die of starvation; for what is she to do anywhere else but beg or starve? She can't take her cottage and garden with her, and she is past work now, you know."

"No, I don't know any thing about it, nor you either, Roger. She may have friends to go to for what you can tell; at all events you ought to drive her away, if you can, before she does any more mischief."

"Very well, mother, I'll talk to some of them in the village to-morrow, and hear what they say. The blacksmith is ready for any thing since his little lad fell sick, and Hodge is the same since poor Cowslip died."

"Very well, then, tell them to give the old woman a good fright. I'll say nothing against that, but give them a horn of strong ale to do it. But, mind, your father must know nothing of this, or he will interfere, and he would rather have you all stood in the stocks, though you are his own son, Roger, than that any thing happen to this old woman, I do believe."

"Never fear, mother, we will keep it close from him. I don't need to be told that I am nothing to my father," he added bitterly, as he left the room and went up to bed.

CHAPTER IX.

TRYING THE WITCH.

MASTER SAXBY walked down to the village the next day as soon as the ordinary business of the farm had been dispatched and the state of the cattle more carefully noted. They all seemed healthy enough now, and Master Saxby hoped he should not hear of any sickness among his neighbors' stock, for he had set himself the task of reasoning the people out of their foolish fears about Gammer Grove being a witch.

The first place he stopped at in his walk through the village was the blacksmith's forge, to tell him of a little job he wanted done, to ask after the sick child, and so lead on to the foolish outcry against Gammer Grove ; for Master Saxby knew that Dobbs was something of a leader among the village gossips, and his forge was the general rendezvous after the ale-house. But Master Saxby had scarcely asked the question about the child before the blacksmith began pouring out his complaints about Gammer Grove and the mischief she was doing; and how he hoped a stop would soon be put to her wickedness, for his little lad was no better, although every known remedy against witch-spells had been tried, and he was then wearing three charms, each of which his wife had been assured was infallible in curing sickness.

The farmer sighed as he listened to the swarthy blacksmith's tale of distress, but still he ventured to say, as the man concluded: "Well, Dobbs, I don't doubt but the child is very ill, but still I cannot see why you charge poor old Gammer Grove with causing this sickness. I am sure she would rather help than injure you."

"Ah, ah, sir, that was when things went pretty much her own way; but we all know she's a Puritan and dead set against Church ales, wakes, and all Sunday frolicking. Since Parson Crane come among us, and taught so much of the king's 'Sport Book,' the old woman has never set her foot inside the church, telling folks the service was half Papist, and she would none of it."

"Well, Dobbs, I myself have heard you say there never was so much rioting and drunkenness as since the Sunday revels began."

"Yes, sir, I have, and I'll say it again; and

not only Sunday, but Monday, too, and half the week the witless knaves are drinking ale and lamb's wool instead of doing their work; but still it is not for me to set myself above my betters, and say it is all through the junketings on Sunday."

"Well, I will say it, and I have told Master Crane the same thing, and that he ought to teach us that the whole day should be kept holy."

"Well, sir, I suppose the king and bishops know best about that, and we are bound to believe them and do as we are taught—leastways that is Parson Crane's opinion, and it suits a good many of us, you see."

"I have no doubt it does; but don't you think a man ought to ponder over these questions, and decide for himself, instead of believing every thing he is told to believe?"

"Well, sir, hammering is more in my way than thinking. I never was much at that. When Parson Hammond was here, of course I was bound to believe what he said—go to church twice on Sundays and keep out of the ale-house, if I possibly could; but now Parson Crane says I may go, and the king will not have me hindered. Why should I stay away, since his majesty has taken so much trouble that his loyal subjects shall not be hindered in taking their pleasure? It is only for us who are loyal," added the man, with a touch of pride in his tone, "for Papists and Puritans are forbidden the privilege of these Sunday sports."

"Well, well, it is useless for me to raise my voice against them, I see; but now I ask you, Dobbs, as an honest man, to do what you can to stop this foolish outcry about Gammer Grove being a witch. You know it isn't true."

"No, sir, I don't; and I can't promise to do more than this—that she sha'n't be interfered with for another week, if you'll send her out of the parish—right away out of Buckinghamshire, so that she 'll never come back."

"But, Dobbs, how can I do that? Would you have her driven away to die of starvation? For it would be nothing less!" exclaimed Master Saxby in astonishment.

The feeling Dobbs manifested against the poor old woman was so much stronger than he expected that he hardly knew what to do. But still he did not despair of being able to modify the opinion of the villagers so that they would, at least, leave her alone, though doubtless she would be shunned and looked upon with suspicion for some time to come.

So from the blacksmith's forge he went on to the ale-house, and called for a mug of lamb's wool to be brought to him in the porch, where two or three old cronies of the village were talking over the much-vexed question of Prince Charles' marriage with a princess of Spain.

"What would our good Queen Elizabeth have said to this Popish match, bringing our blackest foe into the kingdom?" said one old farmer, with a groan.

"Ah, ah, neighbor, you may well say that. When I was in London I went to see Smithfield, where so many martyr fires were lighted, and mainly through another Spanish match, if all is true that our fathers have told us," said Master Saxby, joining the group of gossips.

He was eagerly welcomed, and the latest news he had brought from London, and the opinions he had heard there about this distasteful marriage of their future king, were warmly discussed. It was with some difficulty he could introduce the subject he had so much at heart just now—poor old Gammer Grove, and the charge brought against her. Then he found that these old folks had not troubled themselves much about her.

"She may have made a bargain with the devil, as the youngsters are saying, but it need not trouble us that I see," said one jovial old man.

"Not if she leaves our cattle alone, and don't use her witch spells against any of us; but neighbor Saxby, I have heard, has lost one of the finest cows in the country side through the old woman's arts, and so—"

"Nay, nay, I never said she killed poor Cowslip," interposed Master Saxby; "I don't believe the old woman would do any one an ill turn," he added.

"Well, that may be, and it may not," said one; "but you can't deny that she's always been strange and unsociable like, unless it was at a time of sickness, and then I've thought, may be that being her own evil work, she wanted to come in and see it, to say nothing of its screening her from all suspicion."

"Prithee, now you come to talk of it in that way, nothing is more likely," said a third burly farmer, "and though nothing in the way of polygamy or infanticide could be proved against the sectaries who used to meet in her barn, before they were driven out of the parish, depend upon it there was much evil done among them, and old Gammer

Grove has been practicing their arts again of late."

" Nay, nay, good neighbors, be just even in your anger against the poor old gammer. No one could ever say these sectaries or Brownists were other than sober and industrious folk, and you know that, as justice of the peace, I went more than once to see what was done at their meetings, of which I had received complaint; but I never saw or heard aught but what would profit any Christian man to follow. Praying and reading God's word, with some simple exhortation to live as became the children of God, was all that took place in Gammer Grove's old barn."

" Ah, ah, Master Saxby, these Brownists, or Independents, as they loved to call themselves, were too cunning to practice any evil deeds with a justice of the peace present; but, depend upon it, there was some truth in the tales that were talked about them, or else why did they not go to church? for Parson Hammond was as much a Puritan as themselves."

" Well, neighbor, I never had any complaint about these sectaries except in the matter of their not going to church, and their holding meetings in Gammer Grove's old barn; but as that has been pulled down long since, and these Puritans gone beyond the seas, I don't think we can charge the gammer with their doings. So I hope we shall all be fair and just in our dealings with her as becomes Englishmen."

"Ah, ah, we'll be fair enough with her, neighbor Saxby," said one or two, as Master Saxby turned away. He had another visit to pay after leaving the ale-house porch, and he hoped if he could win over those whom he would see next, Gammer Grove might be freed from any further molestation. It was a small farm at the further end of the village, and the three grown-up sons who did all the work of the place were the most successful at the running, wrestling, and vaulting matches for miles around. This gave them no inconsiderable influence among their compeers of the village.

But Master Saxby's hopes on this score were dashed to the ground as soon as he reached the farm-house door.

" Here is Squire Saxby himself. Now, Job, go and fetch the two chickens!" exclaimed the farmer's wife before a word of greeting could be exchanged.

" How now, dame, what is the matter?" asked Master Saxby, stepping into the clay-floored keeping-room, whither she led the way.

"Two of my best fowls, Master Saxby, have been killed in the night, and no mortal hand has touched them, for not a feather has been ruffled ; they've just dropped dead from the perch like stones."

"I am very sorry," began Master Saxby.

"Sorry!" interrupted the dame, seizing the chickens as her youngest son brought them in. "Look here, don't that look like witch's work?" she said, turning them over in her hand ; "fine, plump young things, as brisk as any of them when I fed them last night, and stone dead in the hen-house this morning."

"They must have been taken with the cramp or the pip," ventured her visitor.

"The cramp!" scornfully exclaimed the angry dame. "I shall begin to think the village is right, and that you are under the old witch's spells. But, squire," she said, suddenly changing her tone, "this can't go on. It must n't be said we are harboring a witch here in Great Kimble, that has always been loyal to Church and king, although there have been sectaries and Puritans among us."

"Well, dame, but I think—"

"Squire Saxby, it wont do to think now ;

you must do something to get rid of that old witch, Gammer Grove. We all knew she was a sectary and a Brownist long ago, and no doubt they are all in league with the Evil One; but now we can prove it against her, and she must leave Great Kimble."

" But—but if we drive the poor old woman away from here, where is she to go?" asked Master Saxby.

" O, never fear but the devil will take care of his own. But go from here she must," concluded the farmer's wife.

" Very well, dame, bring your complaint before me, in proper form, next Tuesday, and I will see what the law says about it," answered her visitor; for he knew it would be useless to attempt arguing with an angry woman, and he bade her good-morning, and turned his steps homeward.

He had promised to pay Master Hampden a visit on Sunday, for the proscribed minister was to be there with a few other friends, and a private service was to be held among themselves in the library, and so if it was necessary he could talk over this affair of Gammer Grove with them afterward; for he feared she would be obliged to leave the village, for a time at least, until this affair had blown over.

So, thinking over this compromise, and wondering whether she would be willing to sell him her cottage and little bit of land, which adjoined his own, he took his way to Hampden on Sunday morning, meeting on his way several people going to church who had not been there lately. He exchanged a friendly smile and greeting with most of them, but quite failed to detect how curiously some of them looked at him as they passed. The fact was, this walk to Hampden to-day, after the stir there had been made about people going to their own parish church, was taken as a convincing proof of his being bewitched, and some few, remembering his leaning to and protection of the sectaries years before, went so far as to say that the squire was in league with the witch, and would never do any thing to rid them of her presence.

In happy ignorance of all these surmises Master Saxby spent a pleasant and profitable Sunday with Master Hampden, and before he left a plan was discussed for saving Gammer Grove, and the villagers too, if she would only consent to adopt it, and Master Saxby was returning home feeling that that trouble at least was at an end.

But as he reached the village green, which

he had to pass on his way, he saw a crowd
gathered round the horse-pond at one corner.
There was a momentary lull in the excitement
that seemed to prevail as he first turned out
of the lane, but the next minute hoarse voices
were calling, " Duck her again, Hodge! Give
the old witch another taste!"   Then followed
a splash and brutal shouts of laughter, in the
midst of which Master Saxby pushed his way
in among them to see what was going on.

"Here's another Puritan! another Puritan!"
shouted two or three half-drunken voices, and
Roger Saxby himself, too tipsy and stupid to
recognize his father, called out, " Pitch him in
after the old witch. We've done for Gammer
Grove, and we'll serve all Puritans alike."

"Go home, sir, this moment! Is this what
you learn from the king's 'Sport Book?'" and
Master Saxby spoke in such a tone of command that the drunken, silly crowd fell back,
and Roger recovered himself sufficiently to
slink away and stagger homeward.

To rescue Gammer Grove, and send one of
the crowd for help from the ale-house, was the
work of a very few minutes; but it was too
late to be of any use. The poor old woman
was dead before she was taken out of the
water, and Master Saxby could with difficulty

Trying the Witch.

get any one to carry her away from the edge
of the pond to the solitude of her own cottage; for no one cared to touch her now she
was dead, although they had been ready enough
to drag her from her home an hour before.

Before they began to disperse Master Saxby
informed them that a coroner's inquest would
be held on the poor old woman, and some of
them would probably be charged with murder,
a threat sufficient to sober one or two among
them, who forthwith began protesting they
had only done as Dame Saxby bade them—
there was no other way of getting rid of the
old witch. Master Saxby did not pay much
heed to these protestations now, but he went
home feeling sad enough for the share Roger
had taken in this cruel business.

CHAPTER X.

THE PILGRIM FATHERS.

THE inquiry into the death of Gammer Grove was not very satisfactory in its result. The belief in witchcraft was so general in those days, and public opinion in Great Kimble had been so deeply aroused against the poor old woman, that her murder was held to be almost justifiable, although the coroner warned the accused that they ought to have given notice to the justice of the peace, and proceeded against the deceased in due form. There was also another difficulty in the way of justice being done. Half a dozen of the ringleaders in the crowd had been arrested, but every body was so tipsy before the outrage had even been thought of that no one could say who had proposed it, or who had actually caused her death. They were half ashamed of the cowardly deed now, and certainly, but for the Church ales they had been drinking it would never have been perpetrated.

But though little satisfaction was given for poor old Gammer Grove, a great deal of ill-

feeling was roused against her friend, Master
Saxby, for taking up her case so warmly; and
whispers were rife about his being under witch-
spells, and more than half a Brownist, and in
league with the witch. Dame Saxby, too,
found her position any thing but an enviable
one, for her neighbors looked upon her with
sly suspicion, as having roused the persecution against Gammer Grove, and then turned
against them for having carried out her wishes
only too well in getting rid of the old woman;
for Dame Saxby, when she heard of the death,
was most vehement in denouncing its cruelty,
reproaching Roger for his share in it as strongly as her husband reproached her for having
first set the rumor afloat that the old woman
was a witch.

And so the winter of 1619 passed slowly
away, bringing but one letter from Harry, just
after he reached Prague. News traveled slowly and uncertainly in those days, and it was
not until the middle of February, 1620, that
news reached Great Kimble of the crowning of
the king's son-in-law as king of Bohemia and
head of the Protestant cause in Germany, and
with it came news of his utter defeat at the
battle of Prague, and that the Palatinate, as
well as Bohemia, was wrested from his grasp.

The news ran through England like an electric shock, and showed how deeply rooted was Protestantism in the heart of the nation; for the murmurs of discontent against the king's policy ran so high that, in deference to this, James was obliged to promise to summon another Parliament, and Master John Hampden was chosen to share the danger of those who were determined to compel the king to do something to help the Protestant cause on the continent.

There was a stir and bustle in many an English household that spring, for hundreds of gentlemen were following Harry Saxby's noble example, and, without waiting for the king's tardy movements, were going at their own expense to join in the struggle for religious liberty.

In this universal unrest Master Saxby felt that he could not stay at Great Kimble. Anxiety to know the fate of his dearly-loved son made him long to be in London, where he might meet some one who had seen him or fought by his side; and so, when the affairs of the farm were set in order so that they might be left to Roger's management for a few months, Master Saxby, with his wife and younger son, removed to London and took lodgings in a pleasant house overlooking the Thames and within easy reach of Master Milton's, whom he often visited of an evening when the scrivener's work was over.

Among the Puritan friends meeting at Master Milton's he heard that a vessel was to sail from London in July, carrying some emigrants who were to join their friends from the Lowlands at Southampton. Shortly afterward Master Saxby went to look over the "Mayflower," as the little vessel was called. Various places had been suggested to the travelers as their future home; the Prince of Orange wishing them to join the Dutch settlement of Amsterdam merchants, on the River Hudson. But arrangements had now been entered into with the Virginia Company for their settlement at a place sufficiently remote from those plantations, that the religious difference between the settlers should not be a cause of quarrel, and yet that they should still be under the British crown; as one of those who had been in the Lowlands, and was about to sail with the little company of emigrants, said to Master Saxby.

" It is grievous to us to live from under the protection of the State of England, for we are likely to lose our language and our very name of English. In Holland, too, we could do but little good, for we could never persuade them to reform the Sabbath, while our children could never be educated as we ourselves had been ; and so, if God be pleased to discover some place unto us in America, we may show our countrymen, no less burdened than ourselves, where they may live, and, being free from antichristian bondage, may keep their names and nation, and not only be a means to enlarge the dominions of the English State, but the Church of Christ also."

"Ah, ah, and many, I doubt not, will follow your brave example," exclaimed Master Saxby. " I would that I could go with you," he added the next minute, with something of a sigh as he thought of Harry fighting in the German war, and Roger, who had of late been such a source of anxiety to him.

A letter had come from Harry lately, telling of his escape after the battle of Prague, but no word of his probable return ; and Roger, he feared, cared less for the Sabbath than ever, unless it was as a day of rioting and drunkenness. It was well that Master Saxby had the affairs of these emigrants to interest himself in, and that many of them were poor—almost ruined through the fines that had been imposed upon them—making them all the more Master Saxby's friends ; many a gift which he thought might be useful to them on the voyage, or when they reached the strange, desolate shores of America, was added to their slender store through Master Saxby's kindness.

He would go with them to Southampton, too, and see his old friend, Robert Cushman, and his family, who were coming from Holland in the " Speedwell," as the two vessels were to sail to America in company. It was near the end of July, 1620, that the " Mayflower " sailed from London with its party of emigrants and a few friends who wished to see the whole party depart from Southampton. The " Speedwell " had not reached its destination when the London party got there, but in a day or two she arrived safely from her voyage across the sea. Then it was found that there were about one hundred and twenty to sail in the two vessels. Robert Cushman was of the number, and right glad he was to see Master Saxby and two or three other friends who had come to bid them a last farewell.

" You will not cast in your lot with us ? " said Cushman, grasping his friend's hand, as they stood on the shore watching the sunlit waves as they danced and rippled round the prow of the little vessel.

" Not now, not now, friend ; but I may come
by and by.   If it were not for the Saxby lands
I know not whether I would not join your
company or go to the German war and fight
beside my son.   You have brought me no
tidings of him," added Master Saxby ; for,
somehow, he had thought that coming from
beyond the sea, these friends must have heard
of Harry, and he had indulged the hope that,
coming to Southampton, he should surely see
some one who had seen him lately.

But Master Cushman shook his head.   " God
grant we may make another England beyond
the sea, where there shall be no more religious
wars," he said, and then he added more brisk-
ly, " But, my friend, why should your land be
as a fetter binding you to bondage ?   Many
among us had lands and goodly houses and
honorable names, but we have forsaken all for
that Christian liberty that is denied to us
here."

" Ah, ah, but you know not all concerning
our Saxby lands," replied his friend ; for, somehow, his superstitious fears concerning the
threatened curse had increased since the death
of poor old Gammer Grove, though why he
should connect the one with the other it was
hard to say.

It was arranged that a parting service should be held just before the vessels finally sailed, and at that meeting a letter, or, rather, an address, should be read that had been given to some of them just before leaving Leyden by their minister, Mr. Robinson, already known as the " Father of the Independents," although he did not follow entirely the doctrine of Brown, whose name was properly given to the sect.

Master Saxby hardly knew what to do about going to this meeting, for his leaning toward " sectaries," who were looked upon askance even by the Puritans of the Church, had already got him into such ill odor among his friends at home that he had resolved to keep more aloof from them in future. But his friendship for Cushman and one or two others of the party overcame his timidity at last, and right glad he was afterward ; for, as he told Master Milton and his friends when he returned to London, he would not have missed hearing Robinson's address for any thing, sectary though he might be.

When the little company of pilgrims and their few friends were gathered together and prayer had been offered, one of the eldest of them —a tall, noble-looking man—stood up and

read, amid breathless silence, the words of the
minister who, like themselves, had shared persecution and tasted of every danger and hardship that beset them while presiding over their
little Church in Holland.

" Brethren, we are now quickly to part from
one another, and whether I may ever live to
see your faces on earth any more the God of
heaven only knows. But whether the Lord
has appointed that or no, I charge you before
God and his blessed angels that you follow me
no further than you have seen me follow the
Lord Jesus Christ.

" If God reveal any thing to you by any
other instrument of his, be as ready to receive
it as ever you were to receive any truth by my
ministry ; for I am verily persuaded the Lord
has more truth yet to break forth out of his
holy word.

" For my part, I cannot sufficiently bewail
the condition of the Reformed Churches who
are come to a period in religion, and will go at
present no further than the instruments of their
reformation. The Lutherans cannot be drawn
to go beyond what Luther saw. Whatever
part of his will our God has revealed to Calvin, they will rather die than embrace it ; and
the Calvinists, you see, stick fast where they

were left by that great man of God, who yet saw not all things.

" This is a misery much to be lamented, for though they were burning and shining lights in their times, yet they penetrated not into the whole counsel of God, but were they now living would be as willing to embrace further light as that which they first received. I beseech you remember it as an article of your Church covenant that you be ready to receive whatever truth shall be made known to you from the written word of God.

" But I must here withal exhort you to take heed what ye receive as truth; examine it, consider it, and compare it with other Scriptures of truth before you receive it; for it is not possible the Christian world should come so lately out of such thick antichristian darkness and that perfection of knowledge should break forth at once."

At the conclusion of this address a chapter from God's word was read and a suitable prayer offered, but Master Saxby was thinking little of either. The wonderful address of this sectary, who had been driven out of England, had so impressed him that he could give little thought to any thing else. The broad, Christian liberality that was shown in exhorting his flock to receive the truth from any one who could teach them, so different from any thing he had ever heard before, made him almost forget where he was until there was a little stir in the congregation, and then, as they rose to separate, he looked round upon the little party of pilgrims, whose souls had been fed and nourished on such strong meat as this minister Robinson could doubtless give them, and truly they looked no unworthy disciples.

Brave, resolute, noble-looking men they were, and women too, worthy to be the fathers and mothers of a new, free, brave race. These were no puling, miserable, discontented sect, but the very flower of Englishmen, with all the grand old English virtues, aided by noble birth and gentle breeding in many cases, and strengthened and braced by enduring persecution and poverty for the sake of that liberty they held more dear than life.

The 5th of August saw the two vessels sail from bright Southampton bay amid the prayers of the little company gathered on the shore to see the last of the white sails as a fair wind carried them down the Channel.*

Then Master Saxby turned his steps toward London once more, to tell his friend Milton,

* See Frontispiece.

and Master Gataker, and other Puritan friends, who could only half believe in the Christianity of these sectaries, of the wonderful address of this Independent minister which he had heard at Southampton. But good men were slow to believe in the goodness of any thing outside the Church in those days, even though they might differ from it in many points, both as to doctrine and ritual ; still, the sin of schism was to them so awful that they were willing to endure any thing rather than be guilty of what they held these Independents to have committed. So Master Gataker could only shake his head and deplore that so many good men should leave the Church of England instead of staying within her pale and striving for a further reform in her liturgy and services.

"I have heard it was what many said about Luther; and even *his* first thoughts were not that he would leave the corrupt Romish Church, but reform it," said Master Saxby.

"Ah, but it was too corrupt," said Master Milton, "and would not be reformed."

"Well, well, I say not that our Church is as the Church of Rome, but will she cast aside what still savors too much of Papistry to please our Protestant stomachs?" said Master Saxby.

"I hope so. I hope to see the day when

every vestige of the old Popish service shall be cast away."

" Many fear that day will never dawn, and in despair of this have separated themselves from us, as Luther did from his Church," said Master Saxby, whose leaning to sectaries was decidedly stronger than ever since his visit to Southampton.

The ground of this argument was gone over by these friends, but they failed to convince each other, although they still remained friends; for no one could help liking kindly Master Saxby, whether they agreed with his opinions or not.

CHAPTER XI.

ANOTHER CITATION FROM THE BISHOP.

MASTER SAXBY spent a good deal of his time in Paul's Walk—or Duke Humphrey's Walk—as the principal aisle in St. Paul's Cathedral was called. It was the most frequented promenade in the city, both for idlers and men of business. Here lawyers would meet their clients, fashionable people their friends, to exchange the news of the day; and the pillars of the sacred pile served as advertisement sheets, in the absence of newspapers, for servants wanting places and masters wanting servants.

Here every scrap of news concerning the struggle now going on in Germany was at once circulated; but little satisfaction, however, could Master Saxby glean from any thing he heard, and the hope of seeing Harry again shortly grew less day by day, although he contrived to send more than one letter to him urging him to come home and take the management of the farm into his own hands.

At last he grew tired of the inaction and

10

weary waiting for news that never came—news
of Harry himself—for beyond a few hastily-
penned lines saying he had escaped after the
battle of Prague, no word had come to cheer
the anxious father and mother. So one day,
about a month after his return from Southampton, when he had spent nearly the whole
day in wandering up and down Paul's Walk
and among the booksellers' shops in St. Paul's
Church-yard, he returned home, and his first
words almost made Dame Saxby jump for joy.

"Moll, we must go back to Great Kimble;
we must go back in time for harvest," he said
with a deep yawn.

"Yes, to be sure; I don't know what Roger
will do without us in the busy season," said
Dame Saxby, who was heartily tired of these
pent-up London lodgings, and she bustled
about to get her husband's supper with re-
newed vigor at the thought of so soon going
back to their own bright country home.

"But, father, we cannot go yet—not for a
fortnight at least—for you promised Master
Oliver Cromwell and Mistress Bourchier you
would go to their wedding," said Larry, who
was by no means tired of London yet.

"True, my lad, I had forgotten that. When
is the wedding to be, dame?" he asked.

" The twentieth of this month. We might stay and see the young couple married and begin our journey the same day."

" Master Cromwell will journey to Huntingdon with Mistress Elizabeth as soon as the wedding is over," said Larry.

" Ah, ah, you have heard all the news, I trow," said his father.

" Yes, I know that Master Cromwell has got six sisters, and those who are not married are to live with him and his wife and mother," said Larry.

So it was settled that they should go to St. Giles' Church, Cripplegate, in the early morning, and then, without waiting for the wedding-feast, begin their journey back to Buckinghamshire at once ; for now that he had once decided to go home again, Master Saxby was impatient to get there. He was not satisfied with the last account he had heard of Roger, and he was anxious to see his friend, Master Hampden, again ; for the much-talked-of Parliament had not assembled yet, although people were grumbling more loudly than ever about the oppressive monopolies and taxes, the Spanish match of Prince Charles, and the backwardness of the king in helping the German Protestant cause.

But if Master Saxby was glad to be among his own fields and farm-buildings, his wife was ten times more glad to get back to her dairy and poultry, and take up the scolding of her serving maids again; and Larry, though he had enjoyed visiting the various sights of London in company with his new friend, young John Milton, and his father, still even he seemed glad to get back to his brother and all the household pets. Dame Saxby hoped that during their long stay in London Gammer Grove had been forgotten by their neighbors, and that she should never hear the old woman's name again.

The affairs of the farm had not prospered under Roger's management, and for the first few weeks Master Saxby's time was fully taken up with setting things right, as far as that could be done. But when the busy season was over he went at once to see his friend Master John Hampden, and hear whether any further steps had been taken to call a Parliament together.

Dame Saxby had already paid young Dame Hampden a visit, for a baby had come to brighten their stately home while the Saxbies were in London, and Dame Saxby had chafed sorely when she heard the news that she was not at hand to give her advice and help at the time.

Now she thought Master Hampden would surely be content to let the king's affairs alone, and not run into such danger as Master Pym had incurred at the close of the last Parliament, and she told the young matron the whole story of his imprisonment, as she had heard it from Dame Milton.

But, to her surprise, the young mother, though she stooped to kiss her baby with a look of more tender love in her eyes, said quite calmly, " John and I have talked it all over, dame, and I have promised never to hold him back from what he sees to be his duty by any weak fears of mine."

" Weak fears," repeated Dame Saxby; " but, my dear Bessie, you ought to keep your husband out of such danger for your child's sake, if not for your own."

" Nay, but, dame, do not think I am forgetful of my little Bessie, if I keep not my husband back from what he deems it his duty to do," said the young mother, with a quiver in her voice, and Dame Saxby saw that it was not so easy after all for her to send her husband on such a dangerous errand as attending Parliament threatened to be.

But before this much-talked-of Parliament assembled Master Saxby was startled by a visit from Robert Cushman, whom he had seen sail from Southampton in the " Mayflower." It was a tale of disaster the brave man had to tell, and filled the friends with anxious fears and forebodings for the safety of the pilgrims who had set forth once more in search of a new home.

The " Mayflower" and " Speedwell," carrying the pilgrims from Leyden, had kept together; but before proceeding far on their journey it was found necessary for the " Speedwell " to put back for repairs, and they ran the vessels into Dartmouth. After being detained here some days they put to sea again, somewhat disheartened at the delay, but still hoping to reach their destination before winter set in. They ran about a hundred leagues, losing sight of the white cliffs of their dear native land, when the " Speedwell " sprang another leak, and they were again compelled to put back. This time they came into Plymouth, where, upon examination, the " Speedwell " was found to be unseaworthy, and the captain refused to venture upon the voyage again.

By these delays a month was lost—precious time that the pilgrims could ill afford to lose, now that winter was approaching, and they knew nothing of the climate of the " New England " they were to colonize. But these were not the men to be turned from their purpose by difficulties or disappointments, and so many as the " Mayflower" could with safety convey resolved to go ; and only eighteen out of the hundred and twenty were left behind. The rest sailed from Plymouth the fourth of September, leaving their friends in no small anxiety for their safety and the ultimate success of the venture.

Robert Cushman had lingered at Plymouth for some time to hear if any further disaster befell the pilgrims, or any homeward-bound ship had brought news of the little vessel; but nothing had been heard of them since the day they sailed, and they must be content to wait until tidings reached them from the far-off unknown land to which they had gone. Months or even a year might elapse before news could reach them, for the " Mayflower " was not to return at once ; and unless the Virginia Company should hear of these new settlers from those who were out there, the prospect of which was very remote, for it had been purposely arranged, on account of the religious differences known to exist between them, that the two colonies should be entirely separated, and one placed at some distance from the other.

It seemed that this winter was to be full of surprises, for preparations had hardly commenced for securing fit members for the coming Parliament, which was at length to meet in March, 1621, when a letter reached Master Saxby from Harry, telling his father of his marriage; and, as though this in itself was not sufficient surprise, he had married a French lady, who, with her family, had been driven from her ancestral home in the south of France by the cruel persecution still being carried on against the Huguenots, as the French Protestants were called. Harry took care to explain that his wife was a Protestant, and a most devoted Christian, as well as a gentle, amiable, tender wife, who had already done much to alleviate the hardship of his soldier life. His mother forgot or overlooked all this, and the bare fact that he had married a stranger and a French woman made her forget even her love for him for the time, and she declared she would never own him—never see him again—and the Saxby lands should never be given to the children of this Frenchwoman. All this, and a great deal more, did

Dame Saxby say in her passion, and Roger took care to keep his mother's anger from abating by words dropped now and then about the land passing into the hands of foreigners by and by. He hoped by this means to induce his father to alter the disposition of the property; for although it had come down from the father to the eldest son for generations, it was not strictly entailed, and Master Saxby could cut off his elder son and leave it to Roger if he pleased. From this time Roger made up his mind that this should be done, and he set himself to please his father as studiously as he could. Now that there was little fear of the land ever becoming the property of his elder brother he developed an aptitude in the care and management of it quite unknown before, and Master Saxby could but feel pleased and gratified, more especially as Roger went less frequently to the Sunday revels at the ale-house than he formerly did. It comforted him a little for the disappointment he felt about Harry—for this marriage had disappointed him, and crossed more than one fondly-cherished plan which he and his wife had talked over for his benefit. They had arranged between themselves that when Harry came home the visit they had promised

to pay young Oliver Cromwell at Huntingdon
should be paid, and they would take Harry
with them that he might see the sisters of
Cromwell; and then, what more natural than
that he should choose one of them for a wife?
his father and mother had argued. So they
had laid their plans for this marriage, and the
installment of the young couple in the old
homestead, while another farm should be
bought for Roger, and they would take Larry
and remove to London, or go to this new colony in America, where they would not be
harassed with vexatious fines for non-attend-
ance at church, or be looked upon with suspicion and distrust if they sympathized with
sectaries.

Dame Saxby could hardly be said to sympathize much with her husband in these latter
aspirations. She did not see why he should
not conform to the law and go to his own
parish church, whatever the doctrine might be
that was preached; but as he would not do
this, and she dreaded the fines and impover-
ishment that must follow his refusal even more
than he did, she was willing to do any thing
to escape them, so as to leave the property
intact for their children. She began to blame
herself now for not having tried to conciliate

poor old Gammer Grove, and so have induced her to remove the witch spells in which it seemed her husband was still bound ; for, not content with offending their own parson, he openly avowed his sympathy with Master Drayton, who had been ejected from the next parish for his Puritan teaching, and helped to support him as a traveling lecturer, but he actually permitted him to lecture in one of his own barns occasionally, and welcomed all who liked to come and hear him.

Of course this could not go on long without attracting the notice of those in power, and before the winter was over Master Saxby was summoned to appear before the bishop. The weather was very cold, and the roads almost impassable with snow, when the summons arrived, and Master Saxby found it impossible to reach the place which had been appointed by the bishop by the day named in the summons.

For this delay he was kept in prison for a month at his own charge, and, not being provided with means for this unexpected delay, and unwilling to vex his wife by what he knew she looked upon as being caused by his own folly, he would not send home for any more money, and so suffered much from the cold,

as well as from the damp, unwholesome prison
where he was lodged.

But, so far from yielding on the point for
which he was imprisoned — for he had been
asked if he was prepared to yield obedience
to the bishop in future before he was condemned to this punishment, and had refused
—so far from yielding now, he was more determined than ever not to wound his own conscience by a weak compliance to ordinances
he despised, and to a spiritual tyranny growing
more like that of Rome every day.

He obtained the use of a Bible in his prison,
and would sit for hours poring over the stories
of the old Hebrew worthies, "Who through
faith subdued kingdoms, wrought righteousness, obtained promises, stopped the mouths
of lions, quenched the violence of fire, escaped
the edge of the sword, out of weakness were
made strong, waxed valiant in fight, turned to
flight the armies of the aliens." And Master
Saxby found the promises made good; "for
out of weakness" was he "made strong," and
he could look forward with confident hope to
the day when old England, as well as the New
England a handful of brave men were going
to found, would be freed from the spiritual
bondage in which she was now held, and all

her sons be permitted to worship God according to the dictates of their own conscience.
But the struggle for this freedom must come
first. He saw that more clearly than ever, and
he, too, must do his small part in maintaining
it. Nothing would be gained, but a step lost
in the onward march, if he yielded now ; and
so, looking on to the victory that must come
by and by, he grew brave and strong in spite
of his meager fare and close imprisonment,
and the bishop found that his spirit had by
no means been broken by this taste of the
rigors of the law. He was certainly disappointed, but, hoping that a few words of warning as to what he might expect for a second
offense might be more effective than continued
punishment, he imposed a moderate fine, and
when this was paid Master Saxby returned
home, but not to attend his parish church,
or to turn his back on his friend, Master Drayton, but to give more earnest heed in conduct-
ing his household after a godly fashion.

CHAPTER XII.

KING JAMES AND HIS PARLIAMENT.

SPRING came round once more, and in March Master John Hampden went to take his seat in Parliament, and his friend, Master Saxby, journeyed to London with him to hear all the news about the German war, and make inquiries about the pilgrims who had gone to America, and the prospects of the new colony established there.

The men chosen by the country as their representatives might have convinced the king that they were in earnest, and were not likely to submit even to his kingly authority in the matter of these unlawful monopolies, and the secret favor he was showing to the Papists by his unwillingness to help the struggling Protestants of Germany.

But he thought to intimidate them at their first sitting, and therefore told them they were no more than his council to give him advice; and as to their anxiety about the Palatinate and his daughter, who, with her children, had been turned out of house and home almost destitute, while her husband was feebly maintaining the unequal struggle for the Protestant cause, he was quite as anxious as they were, and—if he could not get the Palatinate restored by fair means—his crown, his treasure, and his blood should be given to restore them.

He then commanded the Parliament not to waste their time in hunting after grievances, but to use all dispatch in voting him the money to commence the war.

Believing the king's protestations, the Commons at once voted him two subsidies, but the king took no step toward beginning the promised war; and seeing this, the Commons began their inquiries about the illegal monopolies on currants, silver lace, and the licenses granted to hostelries which were in the hands of Sir Giles Mompesson and Mitchell, two creatures of the Duke of Buckingham.

But the king was by no means disposed to have his favorite's arrangements interfered with in this way. The country was his estate, and existed for his pleasure, and if he permitted Parliament to meet and advise with him upon its management occasionally, they must be taught that they could not, and should not, interfere with his prerogative. This was King James' view of the situation, and he cut short their inquiries into grievances, and prorogued Parliament until the following November, to give him time to commence the promised war. So Master John Hampden journeyed back into Buckinghamshire, by no means averse to meeting his dear wife and baby daughter again, but more grave, more anxious, than ever he had been before. He had held many conversations with Master John Pym, who had already been in prison for his bold speaking in Parliament, and it seemed to him now that the struggle between the king and country was but beginning, instead of being nearly over, as he had sometimes hoped it was. Which would conquer in the end he did not know, for on the one side was the deep, calm, but ever-growing desire for more freedom, balanced by a reverence for kingly authority, and a deep sense of the duty of obedience to all lawful authority up to a certain point. On the other hand there was the obstinate determination to stretch the limits of kingly prerogative beyond what had ever been assumed by any sovereign before. James aimed at nothing less than being a despotic ruler, while the people were every day growing less likely to submit to it. This hasty dissolution of Parliament, so soon as he could grasp the money voted, was sow-

ing the seed that might yield a bitter harvest
by and by, either to the king or his son, although Hampden hoped, from what he had
heard of Prince Charles, that he would make a
better king than his father, if only this match
with Spain could be broken off.

Master Saxby was returning home again for
the summer, at least, and as they journeyed
along the roads he and Master Hampden discussed these public affairs, and whether it
would be better to seek a home in the new
country at once, or stay and do what they
could to save their dear native land from falling under the tyranny of priestcraft again, of
which there seemed such imminent danger.

Master Saxby's own opinion was, that it
was decidedly his neighbor's duty to stay,
more especially since he could raise his voice
in Parliament, and make one of the band of
brave patriots who had determined to be the
mouth-piece of thousands of their oppressed
countrymen. But for himself he was not so
sure what was the right course to be pursued.
He had been threatened with a second and
heavier fine in case of his non-compliance with
existing laws, and his return to Great Kimble
now might bring upon him a summons from
the bishop and a second term of imprison-
11

ment, as well as a fine of some hundreds or even thousands of pounds; for this court of High Commission, like that of the Star-chamber, rarely allowed a victim to escape until it had ruined him; and ruin meant worse than poverty to his children, for it would bring upon them the unknown power of their ancestor's curse.

Little wonder was it, therefore, that Master Saxby was going back to his home in fear and trembling, or that he longed for the rest and security of some place where he might worship God in peace and quietness, though he should have to work hard and endure many privations, for the wandering life he would have to lead now, banished from his home, if he would save it for his children, was already growing irksome—almost intolerable. True, there was one way by which he could save himself and live in peace and security, but the price demanded was too high—Master Saxby could not violate his conscience, even for the sake of peace and rest and security.

Of course his coming home brought as much pain as pleasure to his wife and sons, for he still absented himself from church, and went to hear Master Drayton whenever he preached in the market-places of the neighboring towns, which soon set the village talking again, and made Dame Saxby glance fearfully and furtively down the road half a dozen times a day in expectation of seeing the bishop's messenger riding up with another summons, as he came that sorry day last winter. This anxious watchfulness on the part of his wife could not escape Master Saxby long, and it fretted and worried him more than the fear of summons itself did.

"If only Harry would come home, dame, we would go away and leave the lads with the land, and you and I would find a home for ourselves in this new colony of America, where we should no longer be harassed with fear of bishops' messengers and fines, but might end our days in peace and rest."

"I never shall know peace and rest again," said Dame Saxby, bursting into tears; "and as to Harry coming home, what would be the use of his coming now with a fine madam of a French wife? She would ruin every thing in a twelvemonth. What would she know about a dairy and our way of managing poultry? and, after all, why should we depend so much upon Harry? there is Roger."

Master Saxby looked at his wife in blank amazement; for never before would she hear of Roger being put upon an equality with their eldest son. This had been his intention when the boys were young, to divide the land between them; but Dame Saxby had instantly and vehemently opposed it. Harry had been her darling always, and her partiality had often been unduly manifest, which, doubtless, had caused much of the jealousy felt by Roger against his brother—a jealousy which, although Master Saxby had regarded it as a mere boyish feeling, had often caused him some anxiety, and first suggested to him the idea of dividing the land.

His wife's opposition, however, had prevailed. She generally did contrive to have her own way in most things, and Harry had been brought up as the heir to the family estates, while Roger's future was to himself at least somewhat uncertain, although his father had always promised that he should be amply provided for. Now that Harry had so deeply offended his mother, it suddenly flashed across his father's mind that his original plan about dividing the land might be carried out now, and he ventured to hint as much to his wife.

She did not notice this part of his suggestion at first, but said sharply, " You must destroy that deed giving the land to Harry be-

fore your death. Let Roger have it. The lad
is steadier now and skillful in managing the
stock, and with a good wife to look after the
dairy, he might—"

"Nay, nay, dame, the lads shall divide it
between them. I always wished it so, you
know, and I will ride over to Master Hampden
to-morrow and get the deed back. It is hardly just to Harry, perhaps, since he was brought
up to expect all the land; but he was ever
kind and generous, and will not grudge his
brother his due share. This done, I will go to
London again; the 'Mayflower' is expected
to return shortly, and the shipmaster will be
able to tell us all the news about our friends
who have gone to America, and whether the
'Mayflower' will take out a second party this
year."

"Nay, but you will not think of going to
this New England just yet. Wait awhile until
Parliament meets again, and it may be that
Master Hampden and some of the other Puritan members may persuade the king to alter
the laws that press upon them so heavily."

But her husband shook his head rather
mournfully. "Nay, nay, Moll, we must not
expect this just yet. Many grievances must be
considered, many wrongs set right before this

can be reached, and, I fear, each concession will be wrung from the king only after much struggling, and it may be much suffering for those who have made the country's cause their own."

"Dear heart! then, if it is to cause so much trouble, would it not be better to yield at once, and go to church in a decent fashion, and listen to the king's 'Book of Sports' and all other things he may command."

"Nay, nay, Moll, did you never hear of the Smithfield fires in Queen Mary's days? They do not burn us now, but there is still some work to do which the martyrs begun. They died to free our land from the pope at Rome, and we must struggle to free ourselves from the popes of the High Commission at Westminster. They did not talk of yielding because the warfare might be long and difficult. They died true to God and what they held to be his sacred truth, and we must live and struggle for our right to hold the same."

But Dame Saxby could not sympathize much in her husband's noble aspirations. Her one aim was to make life easy and comfortable, and serve God after the same fashion if she could; so she contrived to turn the conversation now by some question about the harvest and the storing of the winter cheese, and then, when he spoke of journeying to London again as soon as the harvest was over, she persuaded him to promise that he would not think any thing more about going to America just yet; that he would wait and see how the next Parliament prospered. He could stay with Master Hampden and learn all particulars of this, and visit his friends the Miltons, and then, in the spring, they would pay their promised visit to Huntingdon, and take Roger with them that he might choose one of Master Oliver Cromwell's sisters for a wife. Only, before he returned to London, he must get back the deed he had lodged with Master Hampden, and destroy it.

"Nay, nay, dame, I cannot promise to destroy it. I will keep it for the present; but the land shall be divided between the lads an you will," said her husband, and with this concession Dame Saxby was obliged to be content.

The next day the parchment making over the Saxby lands by deed of gift to Harry was brought home and put away, and then preparations were commenced for Master Saxby's speedy return to London; for although the Parliament did not meet until November, and

Master Hampden would not go up until he
was obliged, Dame Saxby's restless fear, though
she never spoke of it, was all too apparent to
her husband, for him to enjoy any peace or
rest. So, as soon as the principal part of the
harvest was gathered in, he rode away once
more, thankful to escape from his home without a visit from the bishop's messenger, but
feeling sadly like a man banished and doomed
to wander a stranger among strangers for the
rest of his life.

The whole summer had passed, and the
king's promise and the purpose for which he
had received the two subsidies were still unful-
filled. No army had been sent to help the
struggling Protestants of Germany, and all England was filled with the bitterest discontent ;
for it was pretty generally known now that it
was for fear of offending Spain, that mighty
mistress of Europe, and spoiling his son's
chance of marrying the Infanta, that James
had broken his promise to his subjects, and
well-nigh broken many a father and mother's
heart ; for many had given up their sons, as the
Saxbies had, hoping their king would soon
bring the struggle to a close. But now the
war had already dragged through three years,
and many a brave young Englishman of noble

birth, as well as some of her poorer sons, had left their bones to whiten on those German battle-fields. And it was to please Spain this had to be endured. Spain! their deadly foe, through whose king the persecution under Mary had been mainly instigated ; who had since sent against them the mighty Armada with the avowed purpose of dethroning their Protestant queen and handing the kingdom over to the power of the pope. Was it wonderful that the heart of England beat with the bitterest indignation against this Spanish match ? or that one of the first actions of the re-assembled Parliament should be to protest against it ? They drew up a remonstrance, showing the danger in which the Protestant religion now stood from the growth and encouragement given to Popery, both at home and abroad ; for, at the request of the Spanish embassador, many of the laws made against Papists were allowed to fall into disuse. They also begged the king to break off this Spanish match and marry his son to a Protestant princess, and take up the sword at once for the recovery of the Palatinate, which would restore something of the Protestant balance in Europe.

But prayers and remonstrances alike proved

unavailing. The king indignantly forbade their meddling with his government or his son's marriage, and tells them he is at liberty to punish any man's misdemeanor in Parliament during its sitting as well as after, which he warns them he will not spare.

They at once drew up another remonstrance, insisting upon the laws of the country being observed and freedom of debate in Parliament. In his answer the king denied them what they call their ancient and undoubted right and inheritance.

They entered a protestation in their journal in maintenance of their claim, but the king tore it out and once more dissolved Parliament.

But in the intervals of this warfare the Commons had contrived to do one or two good things, which, doubtless, tended to increase the king's wrath against them. They destroyed several monopolies created by royal prerogative, and Sir Giles Mompesson and Edward Villiers, brother of the reigning favorite, fled beyond seas, and were doomed to life-long banishment. An attempt was also made to break the power of the Star-chamber, and check corruption and bribery among judges and among State officials; and the lord chancellor—the great Lord Bacon—was brought to trial before the House of Lords, and condemned to pay a ruinous fine.

But if the Parliament thus scored a few victories, their feeling of triumph was but short-lived, for no sooner were the Houses dissolved than all the leaders were arrested and thrown into prison. Sir Edward Coke, Sir Robert Phillips, Pym, Selden, and Mallory were committed to the Gate-house. The Earls of Oxford and Southampton were sent to the Tower, while others were banished to Ireland. Little wonder was it that Hampden and several others who narrowly escaped a similar fate should return home depressed and dismayed at these high-handed acts of semi-despotism. What would be the end of such a struggle as this?

CHAPTER XIII.

AT THE SIGN OF THE SPREAD EAGLE.

SIX years have passed since the close of our last chapter—six years of alternate hope and bitterest disappointment for England, and for Master Saxby, as well as for thousands of others. King James had been called to render an account of his stewardship in 1625, and the nation hoped that the young King Charles would rule them wisely and well, in spite of his having taken a Roman Catholic princess for a wife; for although the Spanish match, which had so long been a nightmare to the whole nation, was at last broken off by the favorite, Buckingham, arrangements were at once made for his marriage with Henrietta Maria, of France, a most bigoted Roman Catholic. But still, although her influence over her husband was, doubtless, very great, Queen Mary — as she was called—cannot be charged with having brought all the evils upon the nation under which they groaned, or even as much as she was charged with in those days; though, doubtless, her extravagance and bigotry helped to aggravate the numerous evils.

This year, 1628, had well-nigh broken the nation's heart and its faith in the king's plighted word.   England would never again be what it had been, and hundreds of the best and bravest of her sons were betaking themselves to the shores whither the little " Mayflower," had gone eight years before.   Difficulties before which less resolute men would have given up in despair had been well-nigh conquered now, and the brave, unselfish Pilgrim Fathers had seen the desire of their hearts accomplished and a New England founded " where they could show their countrymen, by their example, where they might live and comfortably subsist, and, being free from antichristian bondage, might keep their names and nation and be a means to enlarge the dominion of the English State and the Church of Christ also." Their " countrymen " had shown their appreciation of their effort by going out to the new colony in increasing numbers each year, until, at the time of which we are writing, the numbers had reached over a thousand a year ; and these were not from the poorer classes, but mainly from the most educated, thoughtful, and refined portion of society.   The very flower of the English State and nation were thus forsaking the mother country for conscience' sake, and to enjoy that civil and religious liberty that yearly grew less and less possible at home.

Master Saxby and his wife were now in London, waiting for the sailing of a vessel that was to take them to New Plymouth, on the other side of the Atlantic; for the good man had been so harassed with fines and imprisonment during the last two years that Dame Saxby had at last urged their going before they should be utterly ruined; for, in addition to fines, subsidies were constantly being raised without the sanction of Parliament, and monopolies were imposed upon almost every article of daily use, besides forced loans, which those who would not pay were imprisoned for refusing, and those who could not were forced to serve in in the army or navy, leaving their families to starve. The king had threatened the Parliament, which met in March, with " new counsels " because they had dared to force from him his assent to the " Petition of Right," which was to secure for every subject personal liberty unless he had offended against the law of the land. The " new counsels " appeared in the shape of a naked despotism. Every thing short of the

absolute surrender of the subject to the mus-
kets of the soldiery was resorted to, and had
the king any military force on which he could
rely, he would at once have thrown off the
mask and governed without any regard to parliamentary privileges. But his army was new-
levied, ill-paid, and worse disciplined, and no-
wise superior to the militia, who were much
more numerous and were under the influence
of the country gentlemen, who, instead of being
subservient to the king and the commands
which he issued through the pulpits of the
country, dared to refuse to lend their money
unjustly, though arrest and imprisonment followed. Every patriot had known something
of this experience by this time, and it was well
that gentle Dame Hampden and her husband
had counted the cost of his going to Parliament, or he would long ago have given up what
must have often seemed a vain struggle, and
settled down to the easy life which his wealth
and position entitled him to enjoy.

How often had he come home weary, jaded,
almost despairing, to be cheered by the brave,
gentle wife and his family of growing boys
and girls! Had he wanted an excuse to abandon his post and leave his bleeding country
to the mercy of the oppressor, he might have

found it in the demands his growing family had upon his time and care, but neither he nor his friend, John Pym, ever thought of giving up the struggle. It might be a forlorn hope they were leading, for all the remonstrances, petitions, and protestations were powerless to move the king to redress the wrongs of the country, and while the court grew more extravagant and corrupt every day, a more grinding taxation was imposed to maintain it. Who could blame those who, like Master Saxby, fled from the country to save themselves from utter ruin? Master Hampden did not, although he refused to cast in his lot with them just yet. By and by, perhaps, if things grew utterly hopeless, he and his friends, Lord Say, and Lord Brook, and his cousin, Oliver Cromwell, would go to America. Lord Say and Lord Brook were already so far anticipating that time as to negotiate for the purchase of some land and the building of some houses, which were to form the nucleus of a town, to be called after them—Saybrook. But not yet would they abandon their posts.

Master Saxby urged that things could not be worse than they were, for the king had broken his pledged word, and copies of this famous " Petition of Right " were printed by the king's order containing his first assent, which had been refused by Parliament as too indefinite, and omitting altogether his second, which had been wrung from him with so much trouble, and which alone made it binding. Then again, since Parliament had been prorogued, fresh monopolies had been imposed, and several friends on the patriots' side had been won over to the king's party. News had just reached them of the parting of Pym and his dearest friend in Parliament, Sir Thomas Wentworth. Pym was neither to be bribed or frightened into forsaking his party; but it well-nigh broke his heart, and he knew the defection of such an able leader as Wentworth would be a heavy blow to their party. The news of that parting at Greenwich, and Pym's words of warning to his friend, "You are going to be undone, and remember that, though you are going to leave us, I will never leave you while your head is upon your shoulders!" These and all the attendant circumstances of that parting were whispered and treasured in men's minds ; some wondering whether Pym, too, would turn traitor and betray his friends.

But, though this year brought such bitter trials and cruel defections among the ranks of the patriots, it brought them also a little hope

12

and encouragement in the election of Oliver
Cromwell for Huntingdon.   None but Hampden, perhaps, knew the value this plain country farmer was likely to prove to their party.
Some deemed him scarcely worth notice in his
country-cut, clumsily-made clothes, his collar
tumbled and none too clean; but they knew
and valued the opinion of John Hampden, the
finished scholar and perfect gentleman; and
when he told them there was more in his un-
polished cousin than they dreamed of, they
took his word, and Cromwell was admitted to
the special coteries and councils that were
held at Pym's house, in Gray's Inn Lane, and
Sir Robert Cotton's library, in Westminster.
These were the favorite meeting-places of the
patriots, and the latter was of untold value
to them, for Sir Robert possessed one of the
most valuable libraries in the kingdom, and
here they could study points of law touching
constitutional right and kingly prerogative
such as few other books would afford.   All
the remonstrances and petitions in this dire
struggle were but for the re-establishment
of constitutional right, and the patriots were
most careful to abide by the law in all that
they did.

But it is time now that we turn to some

of our old friends gathered at the sign of the Spread Eagle, in Broad-street, for Master Saxby was staying here as the friend of the scrivener, John Milton, as being the only way he was likely to escape fresh trouble. An arbitrary command had been issued by the king ordering all gentlemen having homes in the country to live there and leave London. To compel obedience, tavern keepers were forbidden to sell cooked meat, and no hostelry might supply more than one meal to a traveler.

So, instead of going to Shakspeare's "Mermaid," as he usually did, Master Saxby was accommodated at his friend's opposite; for young John was at Cambridge now, studying with a view to enter the Church by and by. The scrivener was very proud of his son, who already gave promise of being not only a learned, but a rarely gifted man, for he had already gained for himself some notice among his father's friends by the poetry he had written. One hymn, which, with a few slight alterations, now finds its way into many a modern hymn book, had been written about five years before, when he was a lad of fifteen; and now as the friends gathered in the pleasant keeping-room over the shop, Master

Stocke proposed that they should have a little music first, and sing Master John's hymn.

The fond father and mother were nothing loth, and the old scrivener seated himself at the organ, and they all joined in singing "John's Hymn:"—

> "Let us with a gladsome mind
> Praise the Lord, for he is kind,
> For his mercies aye endure,
> Ever faithful, ever sure."

When the hymn was sung the friends naturally fell to talking of the writer and his future prospects, and then of the Church and the growth of Arminianism and Popery, which the new Bishop of London, Laud, was doing so much to promote. Church and State were working together now to put down all freedom of thought and action, and the Puritans of London knew that they had little favor to expect from their new Bishop, whose sole aim was to bring the Church into strict conformity with his ideal of what the ritual and doctrine of a Church should be. He was sincere and devout, but narrow-minded and bigoted; spoke of the Reformation as a deformation, and at once set about bringing back some of the Romish practices that had been swept away.

Master Stocke, the minister of Allhallows,

had received notice to rail off the chancel of
the church, and place a table altarwise within
the rails, around which communicants were to
kneel when they partook of the sacrament, instead of standing or sitting round the long
movable table, as had hitherto been the custom among Puritan congregations. Master
Milton and his gentle wife looked amazed and
shocked. "So soon!" uttered the scrivener.
"What do you propose to do, Master Stocke?"

"Nothing. I cannot wound my own conscience, and the conscience of my people, by
setting up Popery and the worship of the
mass in their midst; and what is it less than
that?"

"Ah, ah, we in country parishes have long
groaned under this bondage," said Master
Saxby.

"Will you not appeal to the Archbishop?
It is well known that godly Master Abbot has
no favor to Arminianism; and these high-
Church notions of Bishop Laud, who would
fain have made himself Pope when he was but
Dean of Gloucester, cannot be borne here in
London."

"I might appeal, but 'tis well known that
the archbishop is in no favor at court now, for
his leaning to Puritanism; and his age and in-

firmities will be an excuse for investing our
new bishop with the power of the primate before he shall succeed to that office," said Master Stocke, with a deep-drawn sigh.

"Then Parliament must appeal when it shall
meet again, in October," said Master Milton.

"The Parliament is determined to proceed
in its impeachment of Buckingham, as the
primary cause of all our troubles, and also of
our helping those who sought to crush our
Protestant brethren of France in their last
stronghold of Rochelle."

"Nay, nay, but we did not crush them, and
we are now about to help them. The duke
has even now gone to their relief; he left
London this morning, to sail with the fleet
which lies at Portsmouth waiting his arrival."

"The duke has gone to gratify his personal
revenge against the French Cardinal Richelieu,
and the most effectual blow can be struck at
him by helping the Huguenots in their last
struggle for religious liberty," said Master
Stocke.

"Ah, ah, when the great duke was friendly
with the court of France we were compelled
to send our fleet against these poor Rochellers,
and but for the one Protestant heart that beat
in every sailor's bosom, England would have

earned for herself the undying infamy of having crushed these noble Huguenots. But, thank God, we were saved from this shame and disaster by the mutiny of our brave sailors, who, to a man, declared they would not fight against their Protestant brethren."

"Ah, Master Saxby, you may well say we were saved from that shame, but what have we done to help the struggling Protestants of Europe," said Master Stocke, as he pulled from his pocket a printed sheet. "The Corantes," it was called, and was the first English newspaper published. It gave the latest intelligence about the German war, and this was all it dared to do; for home politics and the doings of court and Parliament dare not be mentioned. Already several brave men had been imprisoned for daring to question the doings of the queen and court, and the decisions of the court of Star-chamber. But news of the German war was gladly welcomed; for, apart from the national interest in the struggle, so many had friends and relatives fighting in the cause of freedom that, like Master Saxby now, they forgot all else for the time in their eagerness to read Butter's "Corantes."

"We may hear of Harry now, before we go, dame," whispered Master Saxby to his wife, as the minister prepared to read aloud some of the latest items of news. This awful war, which had already raged. for eight years, and was destined to last for twenty-two years longer, had desolated some of the fairest provinces of Germany, and famine and sickness had followed in its train; so that this sheet of foreign news was but the recapitulation of skirmishes, battles, sieges, retreats and victories, sickness and death. Regiments engaged, and the names of some who had died or distinguished themselves, were often mentioned, and once Master Saxby had the joy of seeing Harry's name mentioned in terms of the highest commendation for some deed of heroism, by which a party of women and children—refugees from some neighboring town—were saved from death, by his prompt and brave activity.

But there was no mention of Harry, or his regiment either, to-day, and when a little time had been given to the discussion of what had been read, Master Stocke opened the great Bible that had been placed before him, and read a portion of God's word, so dear to every Puritan heart and lover of freedom—the old heroic days of the children of Israel, when they were ruled by judges, who were first their deliverers.

CHAPTER XIV.

A STRANGE MEETING.

PORTSMOUTH was full of visitors when our friend, Master Saxby, reached there; for the fleet had not yet sailed, but lay in the offing, waiting the embarkation of the Duke of Buckingham, who was to lead them to the relief of the struggling French Protestants besieged in Rochelle. But that embarkation was never to take place. While Master Saxby was inquiring for lodgings at a quiet hostelry in the outskirts of the town, a traveler came in bringing news that the duke had been murdered.

"Murdered!" exclaimed half a dozen voices.

"Ay, stabbed to the heart; but they have taken the wretch, who scarcely tried to escape," said the informant.

"He is one of these Puritans, doubtless, who thinks he has done a good deed, and is willing to be a martyr."

"Nay, nay, friend, these are not Puritan ways, to stab even an enemy," said Master Saxby, warmly.

" But you cannot deny that the Puritans in Parliament meant to impeach the duke of treason, and I know not what," said the man, in a swaggering tone.

"The duke would, doubtless, have been called to account for many things which he has caused to be done against the laws of this realm, but he would have been judged according to law, which the Puritans are struggling to uphold," replied Master Saxby.

"Ah, well, the Parliament is saved a troublesome piece of work, and the fellow might have killed many a better man," said another, carelessly.

This last opinion seemed to express the feelings of most of those present, although several went out at once to ascertain if the report of this murder was true, and gather further particulars about it.

While they had been talking another party of travelers had come in—a young gentleman, evidently just returned from foreign travel, two or three servants, and two children. The gentleman wanted accommodation for the servants, children, and luggage that had been left on the ship. He himself was anxious to journey to London at once, but the children required rest before they journeyed farther, and the servants would bring them on by easy stages a day or two later. While the gentleman was arranging with the landlord, Dame Saxby tried to enter into conversation with the children, but she found they could not speak a word of English.

This evidently surprised and disappointed the elderly lady, and she said to her husband, " They certainly look like English children in spite of their outlandish clothes, and the little girl is just like what our Harry used to be."

Master Saxby glanced carelessly at the children, but something in the little girl's face— in the expression of her eyes, reminded him so forcibly of what his eldest son had been, as a child, that he, too, stooped down and spoke to her. But the child only shook her head and turned to her brother for protection against these strangers; and he, sheltering his little sister, turned such a look of angry defiance upon them, that Master Saxby gave up the attempt to become friendly with them. A little later he asked the landlord who his guests were, and was told that the gentleman was Master Harry Vane, who was returning from Geneva, where he had been studying for a year.

From the servants he learned that their master's family were about the court; his father, Sir Harry Vane, being comptroller of the king's household. So Master Saxby had little doubt but that the gentleman had hurried away in consequence of the duke's death, about which there was no doubt now.

If Master Saxby could only have known that it was himself the gentleman was anxious to see; that his journey to London was but a stage on his way to Great Kimble to arrange for the arrival of the children at their paternal home! Ah, if Dame Saxby could only have known that the little girl, who had so strangely interested her, was her dear son's motherless child, how it would have altered all their plans for the future.

But they knew nothing of all this, and so went on board the little vessel next day that was to carry them to the New World, leaving Portsmouth in greater excitement than ever, and the two children eagerly watching the busy crowds in the streets, and condescending to nod a farewell in response to Dame Saxby as she cast a last lingering look at the dear little face framed in the quaint cap of the period, and pressed against the diamond panes of the casement over the gate-way of the hostelry. An hour or two after the departure of Master Saxby and his wife a servant entered the room where the two children were still standing at the window. " Master Rupert, the horses will be ready at six to-morrow morning, and we may continue our journey an you will; but my master bade that you should not be hurried, and so if you would rest here longer we can tarry until Thursday."

The man spoke in German, and the boy answered him in the same language, with the air of one used to control his own actions and order others. " We will journey forward," he said shortly, and then turned to his sister again. He could scarcely have been more than six, but looked eight or ten years old, and the grave protective air with which he drew his sister toward him was very touching. She laid her little head on his shoulder and looked at him with her sweet blue eyes, and said, in a half whisper, " I wonder what it will all be like, Rupert, this new home? Shall we be strangers there like we are here ?"

The boy shook his head gravely. " I don't know what it will be like, but it *can't* be home, you know; no place can be that any more here, now dear mamma has gone to the bright home above the sky."

" But father said our English grandmother would be kind, and we should live in a nice home where we should never be afraid of rude soldiers coming, or have to move away for fear of the town being burned, as we had to do when mamma was ill."

Rupert sighed—such an old sigh for a child! " I am afraid war is a very bad thing for people," he said.

" But father is a soldier, and mamma told us he was the best man that ever lived," exclaimed his sister.

" Yes, yes, that's true enough, and I want to be a man to go and help my father in the battles ; for I've heard him say it is a noble thing to fight and struggle for the right ; but still I can't help thinking that war is bad, for it killed our dear mamma, you know. She would not have died if we had not been obliged to move in such a hurry, just when she was so ill."

" We won't talk about war, then, if it is bad, for I don't like bad things. What do you think grandmother's house will be like, Rupert ?"

" Father said it was a farm-house, with fields all round it, and a herb garden, and cows and chickens. You will like the chickens, Winny."

" Will they be like our own dear little German hens, with feathers all over them ?"

Rupert laughed. "Of course they will. I suppose English chickens do have feathers all over them," he said, turning to the servant, who came in at that moment.

"O yes, sir, they are pretty much alike every-where," he said.

"Then you will feel quite at home with the chickens, Winny," said her brother; and then they began to conjecture what the house would be like, and the English uncles Roger and Lawrence, and the grandfather and grandmother, who were to be as parents to them until the war should be over, and their father could come and claim them again. Little did they think they had already seen their English relatives about whom they had talked so much lately.

Master Vane was almost a stranger to them, and his servants too. They only knew him as a friend of their father's, who had offered to bring them to England and place them in the care of friends; and in the disturbed state of the country Harry Saxby had thankfully accepted the offer, sending letters and every thing necessary by the hand of Master Vane, and never doubting but that his children would be as eagerly welcomed in his old home as he himself would have been.

It had been arranged between the servants
and their master that they should go direct to
his father's house upon their arrival in London,
and there wait his return from Buckinghamshire, if he was not there to meet them.   But,
in the present excited state of London, it was
no easy matter to reach the Strand, where the
mansion of Sir Harry Vane was situated, and
the crowds of strange-looking people frightened the children so much that when at last
they reached their destination the sight of a
kind, gentle, womanly face quite overcame
them.   The lady happened to be passing
through the great hall, and, thinking she must
be the grandmother who was to be so kind to
them, little Winny threw herself into her arms
and burst into tears; while Rupert, quite forgetting himself and feeling that their haven
of rest was reached at last, hid his face in the
elegant skirt of her dress and murmured, " O,
mamma! mamma!"

The lady looked down at the children and
then across at the servants—strangers to her,
but wearing the badge of the Vanes.

" Prithee, now, tell me who are these children?" she said, tenderly soothing little
Winny, and laying her hand on Rupert's head.

The servant advanced a step or two and ex-

The Children Find a Friend.

plained that they had been committed to his master's charge by an English officer serving in the German war, and he had gone to Buckinghamshire to prepare their relatives for their arrival.

" Poor little strangers! And so you mistook me for your mamma, my boy ? " she said, patting Rupert's head.

The servant explained that they did not understand English, as Rupert looked up wonderingly in her face.

" Can they speak French ? " she said, and, without waiting for the servant's answer, she asked if they were tired in that language, which was in such general use among the ladies of the court now that most of them could speak it quite fluently.

It was his mother's tongue, and the sound of the dear, familiar words again overcame him more even than his fright at the strange crowds in the streets, and he answered with quivering lips, adding that his mother had been a noble French lady.

" Come, then, with me to my own room, and you shall tell me all about your mother," she said ; and she led the children away, talking to them in French, and leaving the servant to dispose of the luggage and find his master.

13

But Master Harry Vane had not returned from his journey to Buckinghamshire, and his father was so occupied by his duties at court, and Lady Vane in as close attendance upon the queen, that little notice would have been taken of the children if it had not been for Dame Meredith, a widowed cousin of Lady Vane, who usually made her residence with the Vanes when she came to court.

To this wealthy, childless widow the motherless children became a well-spring of delight, and they became almost as strongly attached to her. There was a tender motherliness about her that constantly reminded the children of their own mother, while the stately court manners, the elegance of her dress, and even the soft, faded beauty of her face, were a perfect fascination to Rupert. He soon began to understand, even before she explained it, that this could not be the English grandmother who took care of the chickens and made cheese and butter; for this lady had a maid to dress her and another to wait upon her, and seemed to do nothing for herself except kneel and pray in the little oratory that opened out of her private sitting-room.

Rupert and Winifred had been taken there the second day after their arrival, as soon as the lady knew that they had been taught to pray. It was a very beautiful little room, Rupert thought, with its purple velvet-cushioned chairs, and the tiny altar with the silver candlesticks, and the handsomely-bound prayer book lying between; but when the lady led them forward, and told them to kneel and thank God for bringing them safely to England and to friends, Rupert drew back quickly, and would have pulled his sister away, too, but Winny had fallen on her knees, and covered her face with her little hands, as she used to do at her mother's knee.

"And why did not you kneel, Rupert?" asked the lady a little sternly when they stepped into the outer room again.

"My father has taught me never to pray to any image," said the boy. "We are Protestants, and I mean to fight against the Pope and every body that worships him by and by."

"But I do not worship the Pope, dear child. The little crucifix above the prayer book in there is but to assist me in my devotions; and surely we are right in using all the helps we can get to worship God 'in the beauty of holiness.'"

"I have looked into some of the Popish Churches in Germany, and they looked very

beautiful, and the priests were dressed in
robes of white and red, and there were lights
and glittering gold; but my father did not say
the people went there to worship God 'in the
beauty of holiness,' but said these beautiful
things did but hide God and make people forget him; and Master Vane told us the same as
we were journeying to England."

"Master Vane has strange notions about
many things," said the lady. "Not that I
think him wrong in this, or your father either.
You have only made a mistake in thinking my
little oratory like the grand Popish churches.
I am not a Papist, as Harry well knows, but
love the Church of England, and long to see
it restored to something like what our new
godly Bishop Laud believes it will be."

It puzzled Rupert a little to account for the
difference in the mode of worship adopted by
the Church of England at home and abroad.
During his father's visits at home, when his
regiment had been in the neighborhood of
where they lived, he had been accustomed to
go with him to what was known as "the English Church," but there had been no ivory and
gold crucifix, or fringed velvet-covered altar
there; a few plain deal seats, a reading-desk,
and a movable table, where his father and a

few others took their seats at one part of the service. This was Rupert's recollection of that English Church, and being an observant, thoughtful child, he was not likely to forget it or to fail to contrast it with Dame Meredith's oratory, where she spent many an hour of the day, leaving them to amuse themselves in the garden, watching the boats pass to and fro on the Thames, or to be amused by one of her maids, but to no other servant than her own attendants were the children now allowed to speak.

CHAPTER XV.

DAME MEREDITH.

THE movements of Master Harry Vane were of small moment to his father just now. He had seen him immediately upon his arrival in London, and knew, therefore, that he was safe; but the bustle incident upon the murder of the Duke of Buckingham, who had always been the reigning favorite of King Charles, as well as his father, absorbed Sir Harry's attention just now.

He may have heard of the arrival of the two children, but this addition to his large household was nothing to him, and so nearly a fortnight passed before Master Harry Vane's return, but no one commented upon it except his own personal attendants, and they wondered where their master could be. His aunt, who loved her nephew as much—perhaps more than his own mother—did begin to grow anxious for his return, although at the same time she dreaded it as the signal for her separation from the children who had so strangely wound themselves round her widowed heart. The day came at last, however, when Master Harry's footstep was heard along the corridor leading to his aunt's suite of apartments, and he met the stately lady with the same affectionate deference that he had felt for her as long as he could remember.

"You look troubled, Harry," said his aunt as soon as he was seated.

"I am troubled, dear aunt, for these children's relatives will have nought to do with them."

"I am glad, very glad," said Dame Meredith, quickly, "for now I can keep them all to myself, and that is what I have been longing to do ever since they have been in the house."

A smile passed over the grave face of the young man as his aunt said this. "I know not whether this may be," he said, "but I will write to Master Saxby, and tell him how ill I have sped on my errand to his home."

"His father and mother refused to take the sweet children?" asked the lady.

"Nay, nay; his father and mother have gone to America. I stayed some days with a neighbor who knew them well, Master John Hampden, a most courteous and honorable gentleman, who told me much about these Saxbys, and this Roger, who is in possession of the old farm—a churlish and evil man, I trow—he must be."

"Hampden, did you say this gentleman's name was?" asked Dame Meredith.

"Yes, aunt. Do you know aught of him?"

"I think I have heard his name, as well as that of Pym, as a most bitter malcontent, and so I hope, Harry, you will have no more to do with him. I will take good care of the children, and do you return to Oxford without further trouble concerning them."

But the lad—he was scarcely more than a lad, hardly seventeen—although the gentle gravity of his face made him look much older, shook his head as he said, " I want to talk to you, aunt, about this same Oxford business; you understand me better than any one else, I think."

" I trust this holiday trip to Geneva has not put you out of conceit of your own university, Harry," said the lady.

"Nay, nay, aunt, you know I never had any liking for the society I met with there, and you, yourself, said my father did but send me that I might forget the serious thoughts I have had of late, and deny the Lord who hath redeemed me from the sin and the evil of the world."

"Well, well, Harry, your father does not understand these matters, but he wishes you well, and fears such seriousness will stand in your way at court."

"I shall never be a courtier," said Harry decidedly, "for I cannot take the oath of allegiance and supremacy even to matriculate, and—"

"Harry, Harry, anger not your father by such whimsies; nay, it is worse, 'tis next to treason to refuse allegiance to your king," said the lady, excitedly.

"I was afraid it would grieve you, aunt, to hear what I had to say;'but you understood all my doubts and fears and hopes and—"

"Yes, yes, your desire to live a pure and godly life I understand well enough, and I have told your father and mother that they ought to thank God that you have given up the follies of the world, and run not to the excess of riot so many do in these days; but this, Harry—I cannot understand this whimsey," and the lady shook her head sadly.

Harry Vane looked scarcely less distressed, for he loved his aunt very dearly, and it was mainly through her influence and example that he had been led to decide for God thus early; but while Dame Meredith had been living with her prayer book and oratory, and giving herself up to the teaching and guidance of Bishop Laud, her nephew had been watching another pattern of the " beauty of holiness " differing altogether from the bishop's ideal concerning rites and ceremonies and ritual. His friend and school-fellow, Arthur Hazelrig, had introduced him to Puritan friends, and now this short stay with Hampden and Pym had confirmed him in his liking for the plain, simple, unadorned service of the Puritans, while the lives and bearing of the men he had met with among these new friends, contrasting so strongly with the self-seeking displayed by almost all he had ever met before, could not but impress the deeply-observant mind of young Vane.

But trouble would come of it he knew. His father was fully aware of his rare ability, and was anxious that he should push his fortunes at court as soon as possible, and he had been sent to Oxford to learn a few fashionable vices, that he might hold his own among the witty young court gallants. But a residence of a few months as gentleman commoner had been enough for Harry, and his trip to the continent had only made him more anxious to spend a year at Geneva instead of Oxford. He wanted his aunt to undertake the difficult business of winning his father's consent to this plan.

"But I don't like it myself, Harry," said the lady, after he had spent some time explaining and persuading her to see things as he did. " All these Puritans talk about is the making of our beloved Church after the pattern of that at Geneva, and your friendship for these malcontents will not fail to anger your father, especially if he should hear of your visit to this Hampden. I believe he was one of those imprisoned for refusing the king's loan, and only lately released."

"Yes, he was one of those brave men," quietly answered Harry.

. "Brave you call it! I should say disloyal," retorted his aunt.

"Now, aunt, don't you be angry with me. You have always been my good friend, and I trust to you to smooth the way with my father. I wish you could see and know this Master Hampden and his friend Pym," he suddenly added.

"Why should you wish it? Is not one malcontent enough in a loyal family?"

"You would not call them malcontents if you could only see and know them. I did wish you could kneel with me when all the

family gathered together in the keeping-room
for prayers and reading God's word. It seemed
like the patriarchal times over again, when the
father was the king and priest, and brought
all his family and servants to receive God's
blessing. The lives of these men are in accord
with their prayers ; and so far from being
law-breakers, they do but seek to uphold the
law against those who would trample it under
foot."

" Harry, Harry, I believe you are more than
half a Puritan yourself," said the lady in
dismay.

" Dear aunt, you would be the same if you
had seen what I have," said Harry, without
denying the imputation. She looked at him
in his handsome slashed doublet and long,
curling hair, and thought what heights of fame
and honor he might reach if only he were more
pliant, more yielding and worldly ; but she
knew him well enough to feel assured that if
once he ranged himself on the side of the
" country party," as it was called, wealth,
honor, fame, ease—all that could tempt a man
in this life — would be spurned at the dictates of conscience ; and she set herself at
once to the task of undoing the mischief she
feared had already gone too far. This visit to

Hampden about the young Saxbys had brought down the wavering balance on the wrong side, and she must rectify it if she possibly could. So she appealed to the lad's loyalty and personal liking for the king, and his love for mother and father and brothers and sisters, whose interests would all be injured, she said, if he ranged himself among the enemies of the king and court. But, although he was deeply touched, young Vane could not be brought to yield. " It is as much a matter of conscience and of right as serving God. Nay, nay, it is serving God in another way," he added.

" But what have these men to complain of? " demanded Dame Meredith. " We have plentiful harvests, our commerce is large and flourishing, and if taxes are somewhat high, the people can afford to pay them, for they never were so well off before as they are now. What have they to complain of, Harry? " she repeated.

" Why, this, aunt, that they are slowly but surely being robbed of their liberty ; that the king assumes more and more power to himself as the right of his prerogative, and the whole realm is treated as though it were an estate to be farmed for his benefit ; and last, but not least, that the Reformation in England has been arrested before it has accomplished all that it has done for the Church of Geneva in purifying it from Roman mummeries."

"But, my dear, our learned and holy Bishop Laud says that much that was done by these Reformers in the days of King Harry was a deformation, and he would fain bring back—"

"The Roman ritual," interrupted Harry. "I heard of the rejoicing at Rome, and how the Pope was preparing to welcome us as a Roman Catholic nation once more."

"My dear, the Pope is mistaken, but it is not very wonderful, for Queen 'Mary here made the same mistake, while others felt equally afraid of what the bishop was teaching; but men's minds are set at rest now, for it is only in a few outward observances that he would alter our Church services to make them accord with that ' beauty of holiness ' he is so anxious to bring back to our beloved Church. Ah, if the good bishop could only have his way in every thing!" sighed the lady.

"He and the king would divide the power between them. He would uphold the king in all his unconstitutional attempts to rob the people of their civil liberty, while the king would aid him to create himself another pope in spiritual matters. A whisper of this has already gone abroad ; that he will take Buckingham's place as the king's adviser ; but they must be careful, for such men as Hampden and Pym and Sir John Eliot are not to be trifled with, and liberty is dearer than wealth or fame to any true Englishman."

Further conversation, however, was stopped by a little cough from Rupert Saxby, which was the first intimation they had received of the children being in the room. Harry Vane held out his hand and beckoned the boy forward. " How would you like to stay here, Rupert, with this lady ? " he asked.

The boy looked at him, and then at Dame Meredith. " I should like to go to my grandam, I think. Winny wants to see the cows and hens," he said.

" Winny shall see cows and hens and have a little white lamb to play with when we go to Raby Castle," said the lady, coaxingly, and drawing Winny close to her.

" Will it be my very own ? " whispered the little girl, raising her sweet mouth to be kissed.

" Yes, darling, your very own. You will stay with me always, wont you ? " almost begged the lady.

For answer, Winny threw her arms round

the lady's neck, whispering, "Yes, I will stay,
if Rupert may stay with me."

"And what says Master Rupert?" asked
Harry Vane, looking into the boy's grave, earnest eyes.

"My father said I was to go to my grand-
dame," said the boy, dubiously.

"Yes, my lad, he did; and I would have
taken you ere now, as I promised your father,
but these good friends of yours have gone to
America. I saw a noble gentleman, their
neighbor and friend, who told me all about it.
Master Hampden knew your father too, and I
have promised to take you to see him one day;
but, for the present, it must content you to
abide here with your sister. This dear lady,
my aunt, will take good care of you both.
Will it content you to stay?"

"Would my father wish it, sir?" asked Rupert, thinking of Dame Meredith's oratory,
which he persisted in esteeming a popish
chapel.

"Yes, my boy, I am sure your father will be
glad to hear you have found a good home
and kind friends in England, for he cannot
take care of you himself in Germany, while
he is fighting with the brave King Gustavus
Adolphus."

"And may I learn to be a soldier while I am here?" asked Rupert.

"I hope you will learn many things besides the duty of a soldier, my boy; my aunt will see to all these things for you," added Harry Vane.

"But I must learn to be a soldier to help my father in the battles; for he is fighting for the truth of God and liberty of conscience, as well as for the elector against the Pope and emperor," said Rupert, quickly.

"Well, my boy, if this long war lasts so long, I hope you will be a brave true soldier, like your father; but, you know, that since the brave King Gustavus has come to their help they have gained so many victories that we are hoping this dreadful war will soon be over, and then your father and many other English gentlemen will return home."

"If it will content you better you shall learn the use of sword and single-stick and all martial exercises," said Dame Meredith; "and at our castle of Raby you will meet with many old men who have been soldiers, like your father, and they will teach you many things of that kind an you want to learn."

"And you shall see my pretty white lamb, Rupert," added his sister, from her cozy seat on Dame Meredith's lap.

14

So the matter was settled, and so far rati-
fied by the children themselves. A week or
two later Harry sent a letter by special messenger to Captain Saxby, telllng him of his
parents' departure for the new colony of America, and the adoption of the children by his
aunt, until he could return and claim them;
adding, however, that he had at last gained his
father's permission to spend a year at Geneva,
and would bring the children with him when
he journeyed thither if he wished it; at the
same time advising that they should be left
with their kind friend, as they were very happy
and well content to stay.

CHAPTER XVI.

HARRY VANE.

CAPTAIN SAXBY heard of the departure of his parents for the new colony in America before Master Harry Vane's letter reached him. Master Saxby had written a day or two before he left England, and the letter had followed the march of the conquering army of Gustavus Adolphus, but at rather a slow rate; so that it was only a short time before Harry Vane's messenger reached him that his father's letter came to hand.

Of course, he could not have his children with him, and so he wisely decided to let them remain with their new-found friends. Before, therefore, Harry Vane departed for Geneva Rupert and Winny went with Dame Meredith to Raby Castle, in Durham. But they did not remain there long, for Dame Meredith fancied it did not suit little Winny to live in the bleak North, so they removed to London again, and then to the lady's own house, at Hadlow, in Kent, where the Vanes also had a country-seat, and where the children usually resided.

They were living here when Harry returned
from Geneva the following year, bringing news
of their father and the German war, but little
hope of its speedy close as yet.   The day that
he arrived Winny was in sad trouble.   She had
been helping Dame Meredith in washing and
clear starching that lady's laces and ruffles, and
now her little fingers were smarting and tingling
from the soap.   Dame Meredith was trying to
soothe her, and allay the pain of her inflamed fingers, when her nephew Harry was announced.

"Why, how now, my little wench," said the
young man, stooping to the little girl as she
sat in his aunt's lap.

Dame Meredith seemed upon the point of
crying, too, as she held up the little inflamed
fingers for him to look at.

"Did you ever see any thing so dreadful,
Harry?   And it is all through that new soap
that we are obliged to use."

"New soap," repeated Harry Vane in some
bewilderment.

"Yes, my dear, have you not heard what an
ado all the washerwomen are making about it?
Last week the Lord Mayor and governor of
the Tower had two grand washing-days at
Guildhall, one day with the old soap and the
next with the new."

Harry looked at his aunt for a minute, as if to assure himself that he heard aright, or that it was his same sensible aunt speaking to him, and then burst into a hearty fit of laughter.

"It is nothing to laugh about, Harry—this monopoly upon the soap"—she said, "for we cannot buy any other now; and just look at this poor little wench's fingers," and Winny, finding so much pity was forthcoming on her behalf, burst into a fresh flood of tears.

"Hush, hush, my little wench, that nice cooling balsam will make your fingers well," said Harry Vane, offering to take the child on his knee. But she clung the closer to Dame Meredith, who kissed and fondled her and promised her some conserve if she would be quiet.

"Where is brother Rupert?" asked Harry, thinking this might turn the child's thoughts into another channel.

"Gone," sobbed Winny; "and it's all through this nasty new soap."

"Why, has it washed him away," asked Harry Vane, laughing still.

"No; I have been obliged to send him out of the room because he spoke disloyally of the king," said Dame Meredith.

"And he is a naughty king to make us

use bad soap; Rupert said he was," persisted Winny.

"Hush, hush, little one.　There, go to Dorothy, and she will find you a large apple," and Dame Meredith sent the little girl out of the room.

"I feel almost as angry as the children, Harry, about this soap business," she said as she sat down again.　"It is nothing but lime and tallow, scalding the fingers and destroying the linen, and yet a proclamation has been sent out forbidding any to make complaint against it, or to use any other, for fear of injury to the monopoly."

"And the lord mayor's washing days—what came of them?" laughed Harry.

"Of course they backed up the new soap as the best, and there is a monopoly upon almost every thing now since the last Parliament was dissolved—soap, and salt, and starch, and coals, buttons, and hats, and combs, and twenty other things besides," said Dame Meredith, indignantly."

"And they are likely to last, for I hear the king has determined to govern without a Parliament in future," said Harry, "and several of the patriots are in prison—Sir John Eliot in the Tower."

"How can you call these men patriots, Harry?" she demanded angrily; for this new soap, having skinned her darling's fingers, touched her very keenly; but she was not ready to admit that the king or his council was in fault. "If it were not for these men —Eliot, and Pym, and Hampden, and their friends — the king would not be driven to granting these monopolies; but since they refuse to lend him their money, or grant him supplies and subsidies, what can he do but make it by selling monopolies on every thing we use? and then you call these men patriots!"

"Now, aunt, you are not just to blame Hampden and the country party for these wretched extortions. It is these very things, and the king's illegal use of the royal prerogative, that have provoked their opposition to him. If he will but deal truly, and rule his realm lawfully, he will have no more loyal subjects than Pym and Hampden, and those who follow their lead; for they are conscientious, God-fearing men, who will do the right without fear or favor."

"Dear heart, Harry, I am afraid your journey to Geneva has been of little use in ridding you of these strange notions," sighed his aunt.

"Nay, but I have learned many things at Geneva of which I had little knowledge before, and I would that our bishops would frame our Church after that of Geneva."

"That can never be," said the lady. "Our good Bishop of London, who will, doubtless, soon be Archbishop of Canterbury, is framing our Church on a different model from the schismatic Church of Geneva. He would fain see it a perfect Church, and all men made conformable to it—perfect in the 'beauty of holiness,'" added Dame Meredith; but which really meant beauty of ritual, according to Laud's ideas of what that ritual should be.

"It is a vain dream, dear aunt, this making all men conformable to one Church, even if it could be a perfect one," said Harry Vane quietly.

His aunt looked her astonishment. "You would make all men conform to the Church of Geneva," she said quietly.

"Nay, aunt, I am not sure that I should wish to try, and if I did I am sure I should not succeed," said Harry.

"But—but when a perfect Church has been discovered men ought to conform to it," said Dame Meredith.

"If they could believe it was a perfect

Church, doubtless they would, dear aunt. I have been thinking much of this matter of late, and I believe every man has the right to follow the divine voice within him—the voice of conscience—in this matter. All men will not, cannot, think alike. God has not intended that they should. He has not made two leaves of the forest trees, even on the same tree, exactly alike, or two blades of grass, or ears of corn; and there is the same diversity in men's minds, I trow."

Harry had thought his aunt must have lost her wits when she told him about the Lord Mayor's washing days, but his astonishment was as nothing to the profound dismay Dame Meredith felt at her nephew's last words. Such a thing as religious toleration for any but their own particular Church, was something unheard of. Each claimed this as his right, but denied it to all who differed from him in this seventeenth century, and the bold, brave words Harry Vane had spoken — and which he was not slow to act upon when the time came—looked, to his aunt, like heartlessness or laxity that was most dangerous.

"Well, well," she said at last, "did you learn this new notion at Geneva, Harry?" I thought they wanted all men to worship after their pat-

tern.   Those stubborn Scotch are not of this
mind, for they would fain make all men Presbyterians."

"It is the fault of this age, I trow, dear
aunt, and an error many good men fall into.
Doubtless these Puritan Brownists, or Independents, as they now call themselves—men
who have suffered the loss of all things for
conscience' sake, and left home and friends
here for unknown hardships in the new colony
in America—would fain make all men Independents if they could; but I trust they will
learn true liberty in the land to which they
have gone.   Aunt, I should like to go out to
this new colony in America," added the young
man.

Had he said he should like to turn Moham-
medan, and go and live with the Grand Turk,
at Constantinople, it would scarcely have
surprised his aunt after what she had already
heard.   She was deeply grieved, too.   Harry
was her favorite among all her nephews and
nieces, and she had indulged such high hopes
concerning him, especially since he had evinced
such decided piety; for in her mind's eye she
saw him brave, witty, prosperous, a bright particular star in the court of King Charles, but
moving in it with unsullied purity of mind and

manner, drawing all men to him, and to God,
by the force of his bright example. A pleasant dream this had been to the lady; but she
feared it would never be a reality now, unless
Sir Harry could prevail upon his son to give
up some of these strange notions.

There was a silence between them after
Harry had expressed his wish to go to New
England, and then his aunt said, " You will
excuse me, Harry, now; it is the hour I spend
in my oratory. Come to me again by and by."

Harry knew that it was to pray for him, and
what she feared was his sad declension, that
she spent so long a time in the little chapel;
for he did not go home when his aunt left
him, but went in search of Rupert Saxby.

The whole household seemed in a ferment
to-day over this soap business, for Dame
Meredith's maid had her fingers tied up, and
there were sounds of scolding and grumbling
from the laundry as he passed on his way to
the garden, where he had been told the children were walking. He found them sitting
together in a retired arbor, Rupert trying to
coax Winny to play, while the little girl was
still fretting and complaining about her sore
fingers, which Dorothy had tied up in some
linen rags. Harry sat down on the seat, and

took Winny on his knee, condoling with her about her sore fingers, which at once loosened Rupert's tongue about the soap. Dorothy, as well as Dame Meredith, had scolded him for speaking so angrily against the king and those who had bought the monopoly and made such bad soap; but he gave vent to his feelings afresh now, using no very measured language, either, to express his anger.

Harry Vane was astonished to hear him, and feared that his aunt must, by her over-indulgence, be spoiling the children. Those were the days when children were not merely supposed to be seen and not heard, but when it was an accomplished fact. That it was not so with the little Saxbys showed a great want of moral training, thought Harry Vane, and it vexed and troubled him exceedingly.

Rupert was a boy of fine promise, thoughtful beyond his years, generous and loving, and wisely trained. These good qualities might, by the blessing of God, be made a blessing to others—so ran Harry Vane's thoughts, as he talked and listened to the children, inwardly wondering what he ought to do—what it was his duty to do under these circumstances. He had no love for stirring up strife and opposition, and he feared he should do this only too well on his own account, without offending and paining his aunt by removing the children from her care. Then again, where could he take them, for the slender pittance Captain Saxby could afford to pay for them, if called upon to do so, would not be sufficient.

At length he decided to pay another visit to Master Hampden, and take Rupert with him, and perhaps this old friend of the Saxbys could suggest some plan — might even offer to take Rupert for a time. Rupert was his chief anxiety. A little spoiling would not matter so much in Winny's case, he thought, and so he decided to talk to his aunt about this at once.

Leaving the children to their play, he sauntered back to the house, but still had to wait some time for his aunt, who had not yet left her oratory, her maid informed him. As soon as she came in Harry noticed the calm, peaceful expression of her placid face, that had looked so ruffled and troubled when she left him, and the thought instantly crossed his mind, "how can I say hard things about this ritual, and times, and ceremonies, when I see what a help it is to one devout soul?" Ah, Dame Meredith, when she blamed her nephew for the broad, liberal, Christlike spirit which

she in her fearfulness looked upon as laxity, if
not actual license, little thought how much
her example had to do with planting and fos-
tering it.

"Now, my dear, you will tell me about your
travels," she said, taking a stiff, high-backed,
but handsomely-embroidered, chair, and inviting her nephew to one close to it.

"Well, aunt, I want to talk to you about
another journey I am anxious to take at once,
before my father returns from his mission to
Sweden. You remember before I went away
last year I told you that I promised one of
Captain Saxby's friends that he should see
these children."

"Who is this friend?" asked the lady
quickly. "He will not want to take the children from me, I hope," she added.

"I only wish to take Rupert with me now.
I told you Master Hampden was an old friend
of the family, and I had promised the boy
should pay him a long visit."

Dame Meredith's face grew troubled. "I
wish you would not go to this man. Take
the boy anywhere else you like, Harry—I can
trust you fully—but why should you take him
to this Master Hampden, who is one of the
bitterest of these malcontents?"

"He is his father's friend, dear aunt," said Harry in a soothing tone.

"But why not let the children remain with me until their father comes home?"

"Because—dear aunt, I do not wish to pain you, but there are many reasons why it would be best for Rupert to pay this visit to Master Hampden now," said the young man.

"Then you are determined to take him, I suppose?"

"His father would wish it, I am sure, and, therefore, I feel bound to carry out his wishes."

"But you will not take my little darling, Winny," said the lady almost imploringly.

"No, I will leave Winny with you, and, doubtless, Rupert will return in a few months, or even weeks."

"One thing more, Harry—you will spend Sunday with me?" said Dame Meredith.

"Yes, aunt, if you wish it, certainly," said Harry, glad to please his aunt in something; and so it was settled that he and Rupert should start on their journey to Buckingham-shire the following Monday.

CHAPTER XVII.

BITTER DISAPPOINTMENTS.

IF Dame Meredith and Harry Vane could only have known what painful memories this Sunday at Hadlow Church was destined to give rise to, each would have been most careful to avoid it, but Dame Meredith had persuaded herself that there was, at least, some small good in her nephew's lax notions about men's conformity to the Church ; for if he held that they might worship God after any pattern, he would not be so violent in his opposition to the changes gradually being introduced by Bishop Laud, and surely he would see that the new mode of administering the Lord's Supper was more reverent—more in accordance with the beauty of holiness.

Harry had not been into the parish church since these changes had been made, and he stared in amazement as he walked up the aisle to the railed-off family pew of the Vanes, and saw that a table had been set up at the end of the chancel, furnished like an altar, and separatcd from thc rest of the church by a raised step, and railings around it.

He had no opportunity of questioning his aunt or any one else until the communion service commenced, and then, instead of the long, movable table being placed in the center of the church, around which the communicants stood to partake of the Lord's Supper, he saw, to his profound astonishment, that they kneeled around the railings that guarded the altar-like table.

"Another step and we shall have the mass itself set up in our midst," he said half aloud, as he watched his aunt take her place among the kneeling communicants. Harry had fully intended partaking in this sacred feast, but he could not, would not kneel. To him and to hundreds of others this posture savored too much of idolatry; it was too much like the adoration of the host, and in the recoil from popery and the dread fear of its return which possessed so many just now, they would not yield an inch by which the enemy might gain an advantage.

Dame Meredith looked sorely pained when she saw that her nephew did not go forward with the rest, and as soon as the service was over and they had reached the church-yard,

15

she exclaimed, "O, Harry, Harry, I am sorely grieved! Why did you not kneel with me to-day at the blessed sacrament?"

"I, too, was grieved and sorely disappointed," said the young man with a deep-drawn sigh, "for it seems to me that this Church of England is growing more Romish every day."

"Nay, nay, it is not Romish, but reverent and becoming to kneel when we partake of the blessed sacrament of the body and blood of Christ," said Dame Meredith, quickly.

"I cannot kneel — I cannot worship this bread and wine, as though it were the body and blood of Christ himself," said Harry.

"But—but, you told me a day or two since you believed God would accept the worship of a sincere and devout soul, whatever the form of worship might be," objected his aunt.

"And I do believe it, provided the worship be rendered according to a man's conscience," said Harry; "but I should sorely wound my conscience to kneel for this service where I have always stood; and, God helping me, I never will," he added solemnly.

"O, Harry, Harry! it will sorely grieve your father and the king. You cannot think that so many devout and godly men as follow this way would do wrong."

"I judge no man but myself," said Harry, "and I can believe in the truth and devotion of many pious souls who conform to this fashion, but I cannot do it."

Dame Meredith sighed as she looked at her impracticable nephew, and thought of the trouble in store for them all. She went home and spent an hour or two in her oratory, praying for the high-souled, but, as she thought, wrong-headed young man, who must, by mere force of character, be such a power in the world for good or evil; and as Dame Meredith looked upon those who opposed the king and all-powerful bishop as very evil, she was the more earnest that her nephew should be saved from such wiles. She decided to see the bishop, too, and talk to him about Harry. Surely a few words from him would bring the wanderer back to the fold; and so as soon as Harry and Rupert, with the attendant servants, had started on their journey to Buckinghamshire, Dame Meredith gave orders to her servants to prepare for a visit to London, where she resolved to see Bishop Laud and meet Harry on his return.

Rupert was very sorry to leave his sister, but

the novelty of the journey and the anticipation of seeing his father's old friends and old
home reconciled him to the separation, while
Winny was soothed with a present of comfits
and confections now, and a promise of visiting
the little prince and seeing his wonderful
French toys when they should reach London.

Harry Vane kept little Rupert as near to
him as he could during the journey, often seat-
ing him in front of himself as he rode, although a pony had been provided for the child,
and he had already learned to ride very well.
He took care that he should be so seated and
he rode his horse at a leisurely pace as they
drew near the old Saxby homestead.

"There, my boy, that is your father's home,
and will be yours some day, I doubt not," said
Harry Vane as they drew near the gate.

"That!" exclaimed Rupert, in some surprise, for the old house was falling into decay,
and Master Vane noticed how neglected and
dilapidated everything was looking now. Paths
were weed-grown and untidy, gates were falling off their hinges, hedges were broken down
and showed ugly gaps, and an air of miserable
desolation reigned over the whole place.

"It was not like this when I saw it last year,
Rupert. I wonder whether your uncle has

died and there is no one left to take care of the old place now," and he urged on his horse again toward Hampden, leaving the gossips of Great Kimble in a flutter of astonishment and conjecture as to who the grand visitors could be.

Very different was the aspect of Master John Hampden's residence. The broad avenue, sheltered by lofty, overarching trees, had been clean swept of the falling leaves, and every thing gave token of the wealthy, careful country gentleman, who was proud of his home and its surroundings.

The announcement of his visitor's name soon brought Master Hampden to the door to welcome him, and Rupert was taken at once to gentle Dame Hampden, to be introduced to her numerous family of boys and girls, some of whom were older and some younger than Rupert. Orders were issued for servants and horses to be made comfortable, and refreshments were at once brought in for Harry Vane. This meal dispatched, he began to question his host about the change that had taken place in the Saxby homestead during the last year.

" Yes, every thing is going to rack and ruin under Roger's management," said Master

Hampden, " and, what is worse, he seems to be going the same road himself."

" There are two brothers living there, I think you said ? " remarked Harry Vane.

" Yes, Lawrence, the youngest of the three, was left behind at his own request when his mother and father went to America ; for these two boys were very fond of each other, and were to manage the farm between them until Captain Saxby came home, when the key of an old cabinet was to be given to him—the key, by the way, is in my possession—and he would see, by an examination of its contents, what his father's wishes were about the estate. Roger has never felt satisfied about this, it seems, but he and Lawrence were always good friends until you came last year about the children. They had a serious quarrel after you left—the first real quarrel they have ever had. Since then they have been frequent enough, until at last Lawrence has decided to go to his parents in America. He came to consult me about it only last week, and I think it is the best thing he can do, unless he is to go to ruin like his brother."

" This new colony in America seems the only hope for many of us," said Harry Vane. " Young Saxby may tell his friends that I shall probably take their grandson out with me by and by."

"You go to this half-civilized place, Master Vane! You that have been reared in the luxury and splendor of a court!" exclaimed Hampden.

"Luxury and splendor are not freedom. I cannot even worship God according to my own conscience, Hampden. Do you know a clergyman who would let me take the sacrament standing now?"

Master Hampden shook his head. "We had a brave, true, God-fearing man here a few years ago, in whose defense Master Saxby suffered a good many losses and a good many vexations, but he has been imprisoned by Bishop Laud's order, and there is as little hope of his release as of our friend Sir John Eliot's."

"Your brave leader is in prison again?" said Harry Vane, questioningly.

"Yes, most illegally committed to the Tower by the Council and Star-chamber two days after the dissolution of Parliament."

"What was his offense?" asked Harry Vane.

"The old and oft-told tale, denying the king's right to levy taxes without the consent of Parliament. The matter immediately in dispute was that of tonnage and poundage,

levied immediately after the last Parliament
was prorogued, and in direct defiance of the
Bill of Rights.   You have heard of this famous
bill, Master Vane, and the trouble it cost us
to gain the king's assent thereto."

"I would that I had never heard of it, or
the king's share in that most dishonorable
business," said Harry Vane.

"Well, well, we will not discuss that now,"
said Hampden, with delicate courtesy for his
visitor's feelings, to whom the king was a personal friend as well as a sovereign.   "The Bill
of Rights, as you well know, was to make
clear, once for all, that the State had not absolute power over the lives and property of the
subject, as had of late been assumed ; but, in defiance of this, tonnage and poundage was immediately levied, and three worthy citizens of
London had their goods seized, the judges refusing them protection because they declined
to pay this illegal impost.   When Parliament
met, Sir John Eliot brought forward a remonstrance against this, but the speaker would
have left the chair when it was to be read had
not Denzil Hollis held him down while Sir
John Eliot read his remonstrance against the
king's illegal action."

"And it was for this he called you a nest of

' vipers,' I suppose," said Harry Vane, who had heard of the king's angry dissolution of this Parliament, and his declared intention to rule the kingdom without a Parliament in future.

" Master Vane, we have been no vipers, but true men and the king's most loyal subjects; but if such noble gentlemen as Sir John Eliot are to be imprisoned for speeches in Parliament, the time may come when the king will find us vipers indeed. We are Englishmen, patient and law-abiding, demanding only to be ruled according to law; but if this be refused us and all our rights denied, a day will come when remonstrances and protests will be laid aside and sterner weapons taken into use. I tell *you* this, Master Vane, that you may give a word of warning in time to those whom it may concern—I tell you I *fear* such a day will come, unless the king will take other counselors than Sir Thomas Wentworth, the traitor of our cause, and Laud, the Arminian bishop, who would fain become Pope of the Church of England."

" I fear words of mine will have but little weight with the king or his party. But, can nothing be done for Sir John Eliot?"

" I fear not, although his health is suffering

from the closeness of his confinement. He
has used every lawful means to gain his liberty, but the king demands that he shall petition, declaring he is sorry he has offended."

"And he will not do this?" said Harry Vane
with flashing eyes.

"Do it! Would it not be conceding to the
king the right for which we have been contending so long?—the right of the subject to
his liberty and property, unless he has offended against the law. This Sir John Eliot has
not done; and as for being sorry for what he
said, he would do it again the next time he
stood in Parliament; for what would freedom
be worth to a man like Sir John, if he dare not
raise his voice on behalf of the oppressed?"

Harry Vane shook his head sadly. "What
is coming to our poor England when true,
honest men are shut up in the Tower or banished to Ireland, and traitors like Wentworth
rewarded for their treachery? Master Hampden, we must all go to this New England the
men of the Mayflower have discovered for us."

But Hampden shook his head. "Not yet,"
he said; "not while there is a chance of saving dear old England."

"But, can we save her?"

"We will spend our lives in the effort. Pym

and Sir John Eliot, my cousin Oliver Cromwell, Masten and Selden, Lord Say, and Lord Brooke, we have all sworn to think of our country's welfare before our own, and we will die rather than see her the down-trodden victim of any oppression."

"And I will join you," said young Harry Vane, speaking slowly but firmly.

Hampden looked at the noble, boyish face, and shook his head. "You will ever be our friend among the court party, I doubt not; but to join us—to rank yourself openly on our side, you know not what this will cost you. You have been reared in the midst of the court; all your friends are of it, and to leave these—to give up all your hopes for the future —you must consider it well, young sir, before you decide so weighty a question."

"But I am one with you in conscience and religion, aye, and in politics, too. Think you that, after seeing the Church of Geneva in all its purity and simplicity, I could join this half-Romanized Church that Laud has given us? I tell you I will never kneel to take the sacrament; and if no man will give it me standing, I'll wait until your day comes, or I go to this New England and take it with my Puritan brethren there."

"Well, well, for the matter of that, I blame you not," said Hampden; "but in this question of politics be not hasty; be our friend with the king an you can, but for the rest wait."

"How long?" asked Harry Vane. "If I come to you and Pym in five years' time, and say, 'Here I am, another man for England; I have never wavered since I made my choice—'"

"Then we will receive you gladly," interrupted Hampden.

CHAPTER XVIII.

ROUNDHEAD AND ROYALIST.

DAME MEREDITH sat in the wide oriel window of the Vane Mansion, in the Strand, watching the swans as they sailed gracefully up and down the river, and the boats and gaily-decorated barges, with their company of fine ladies and gentlemen on their way to and from Whitehall. The sun shone through the little lozenge-shaped panes of glass, making quaint patterns on the polished dark oak floor. At the lady's feet sat a little fair-haired girl, about ten years old, with wide-open, serious-looking eyes.

" Madam, will my brother Rupert grow up a very bad man an he goes with Master Harry Vane to this New England?" she said seriously, after a long silence.

The lady turned her face to gaze at the child for a minute, and the tears were in her eyes as she said: " I would give all I possess to save Master Vane from the presumption, and folly, and spiritual pride that has driven him to turn his back upon his friends, and forsake his king and the Church in which he learned to serve God; but for all this Harry Vane is not a bad man, and he will strive to teach our Rupert all that he thinks right and true and good."

"Then there are two sorts of goodness, madam?" said little Winny.

Dame Meredith seemed puzzled to answer the child's question. "There should not be, little Winny," she said at last; "but the times are out of joint, and many set little store by loyalty to the divine right of the king, or obedience to holy Church. But why do I talk to you of these things which you cannot understand? Run to Dorothy and tell her to give you some comfits and take you to walk in the garden. I expect Master Vane will be here in a few minutes."

"But—but, madam, I may see Rupert before he goes across the great sea?" said Winny, doubtfully.

"Yes, to be sure, child, you shall see your brother. He is coming here to-morrow."

"Then I will talk to him of this evil way he is in," said Winny with the gravity of Dame Meredith herself; for, having so little companionship with children of her own age, the little girl had grown up with the manners and speech of her elders, and thought more than most children of her age over what she heard.

The child had only just left the room when Harry Vane was announced, and the next minute stood in his aunt's presence. The four or five years that had elapsed since his return from Geneva had altered much of the boyish expression, but not the noble truthfulness of his face.

"How now, my sweet aunt?" said Harry, doffing his plumed hat and throwing aside his scented love-locks as he stooped to kiss his aunt's hand.

"How now, Cousin Harry? I looked to see thee as a veritable roundhead knave by this time," said his aunt playfully, laying her hand on his curls, and evidently pleased to see that he still followed some custom of the court, whatever his private opinion might be.

"Nay, God is not served by the cut of a man's doublet or the shearing of his hair," said Harry with a smile, drawing a narrow, highbacked chair close to his aunt's.

"Well, now, wherefore is this new whimsy of thine, about which thy father is fretting and fuming? I thought thou and he were close friends since this business at Sweden had occupied you both."

"In matters of business which touch neither king nor Church my father and I will ever be good friends," said Harry; "but since the king will rule this realm without law—"

"And wherefore should not the king rule it as he will? Is it not his right?" interrupted Dame Meredith, sharply.

"An he would rule according to law no one would gainsay it," replied Harry, and then added: "but you and I are not going to quarrel, sweet aunt. I love thee too well to go forth on my perilous adventure leaving thee in anger. I came to talk to thee of these children."

"Thou dost not want to take my sweet bud of promise, Winny, away from me?" interrupted the lady quickly.

"Nay, dear aunt; what could I do with a little wench on my adventure? But the boy is anxious to go to his friends, and they have sent letters to Master Hampden begging he will send them both by the hand of some trusty friend. I will take Rupert, and persuade them to let the little wench abide with thee until her father shall return from the wars, when thou wilt, of course, be willing to give her up."

"Have I not always said I would yield the

little wench to her own father? And now, Harry, a word about yourself; wherefore dost thou continue in this stout rebellion against the king and the true Church? Why dost thou not obey her, and submit to her authority?"

"What! give my conscience to a priest! Nay, nay, aunt, I hold that every man is himself a priest in this matter, and may not delegate the office to another without loss to his own soul."

" I had thought our godly Archbishop Laud would have brought thee to a better mind," said Dame Meredith with a sigh. " How is it thou dost arrogate to thyself a wisdom greater than thy father or mother? Dost thou not think it comes of the presumption of youth and an overweening contempt of authority, which is also another youthful fault, but still not incurable?"

But her nephew shook his head. " Sweet aunt, I thought you knew me better by this time," he said. " To please you and my father I had a long discussion with Laud, but he did not move me an inch from the truth I had learned."

" Harry, Harry, what are you saying? The archbishop move you from the truth! Nay,
16

nay, he would lead you to the truth, vain boy,"
said Dame Meredith.

"I doubt not Master Laud's sincerity, or
that he hath a grip of some fragment of truth,
albeit it is well-nigh hidden from the multitude
by the ceremonies and mummeries which the
Church hath of late imposed. But truth is
many-sided, and we speak that we do know
and testify that we have seen, and wherefore
should I give this up at the bidding of king or
archbishop, for Charles himself hath caught me
more than once on this hap?"

"I would that he had made thee give up thy
headstrong ways, that cause such sore grief to
thy friends," said Dame Meredith.

"Nay, sweet aunt, if you have failed, how
think you others can succeed? But now let
us talk of other things. I would that I had
seen the brave Sir John Eliot before he died,
for he had many friends, I trow, in the New
England to which I am going."

"He died a prisoner in the Tower," said
Dame Meredith.

"Sir John died a martyr for his country,
the victim of the king's tyranny," said young
Vane.

"I would every evil-minded roundhead was
now in the Tower. I would almost send you

there an it would cure you of this pestilent heresy," she added ; and truly the good dame would have sent her dearly-loved nephew any where out of the way of these new opinions that were so slowly but surely alienating men's minds from the king, and preparing them for that final struggle when they would fight with other weapons than those of protests, and re-monstrances, and stern parliamentary phrases, which was all that had ever been thought of as yet by the king-loving, law-abiding people, or their leaders either.

And now the talk of Dame Meredith and Harry Vane was about the voyage across the Atlantic, the retinue of servants and retainers he would take with him, and the need for pro-viding other and more substantial garments than satin and velvet doublets and silver-lace-trimmed cloaks. To his aunt's horror, Harry was bent upon providing himself with several substantial suits of homely frieze and one or two jerkins of buff leather, such as peasants wore, but which would be very unfitting for the court-bred Harry Vane, his aunt argued. But Harry was as determined about the frieze doublets as he was about his religious opinions, only he promised to go on board the vessel in a dress becoming Sir Harry Vane's son ; and this was the utmost he would concede to his aunt's whimsy.

The next day Rupert arrived from Hampden, where most of his time had been spent since he first went there with Harry Vane. He had grown a fine, handsome lad, grave perhaps beyond his years, but then he had been brought up in a Puritan household, and they were hardly the times for much merry-making when any day might see father or friends carried off to prison, and such ruinous fines imposed that the whole family might be reduced to ruin. Such things were only too common under the tyranny of the Star-chamber, and so it was little wonder that those who lived in constant danger of falling into its power under one pretext or the other should take a serious view of life, or that children should catch the tone of this from their parents almost insensibly.

But Rupert had been brought up among young people near his own age, and his little sister's solemn lectures on the evil of following Master Vane's foolish ways greatly surprised him.

" I have seen but little of Master Vane, and shall see less, I trow, when I reach Saxby, on the other side the great sea—New Saxby my

grandfather calls it; and he would fain give
up the old Saxby here in Great Kimble, for it
has done my Uncle Roger much mischief,
Master Hampden says."

"But you must not hold by all this Master
Hampden tells you. He is an evil-minded
roundhead, and would fain take all power from
the king and put our godly bishops into
prison," said Winny.

Rupert looked at her in astonishment, and
then burst into a merry peal of laughter at
Winny's grave face. "So Mistress Dorothy
has been teaching you high things, little sister," he said, catching her in his arms and kiss-
ing her.

But Winny struggled to free herself, looking
very angry. "You shall not love me an you
will not love the king and the good archbishop," she said.

"Nay, nay, have I ever said aught to offend
the king or the archbishop?" said Rupert, in
the same tone of amused surprise; for although
the elder children among the Hampdens may
have known something of these things—remembered their father's imprisonment and
their mother's grief and anxiety at that time
—the younger ones, with whom Rupert had
had his lessons, had heard but little of the dif-

ferences of opinion that rent the nation and families, and often men's own hearts, as in the case of Harry Vane; for it was no light thing to forsake home and friends and every prospect of advancement, even the opportunity of doing his party good, as some whispered, for liberty of conscience. His sister's words were, therefore, the more strange to Rupert; but though he put them aside laughingly he did not forget them, and resolved to ask his friend, Master Vane, all about them, when they were on board the ship. At present they had enough to do, each in his own separate ways, Rupert rambling about the garden and watching the swans on the river, or sometimes going on water excursions as far as Greenwich in the stately family barge, while Master Vane was busy bidding his friends farewell and making his final preparations for departure. They did not see a great deal of him at home; most of his time was spent in Gray's Inn Lane, at the house of his dear friend, Master Pym, where he met more congenial friends than those at home or at the palace of Whitehall. So, except his own family, few of his former associates saw any thing of Harry Vane during his last days in England.

To please his aunt and family Harry went

to the vessel in state befitting his father's position. His rich dress and long, scented love-locks, however were a great offense to his fellow-passengers, most of whom were Puritans, not only in heart but in the cut of their garments and the fashion they wore their hair, and they felt greatly scandalized at their fellow-passenger's laxity in these particulars. When they heard who he was they regarded him as a spy sent out by the government to report upon the state of the new colony. Before the end of the voyage, however, they had another complaint to bring against this strange young gentleman, not on the score of laxity, for, in the words of an old chronicler we read, " But he that they thought at first. sight to have too little of Christ for their company did soon after appear to have too much for them."

What a wonderful voyage that was for young Rupert Saxby! Harry Vane, whom his fellow-passengers turned from in coldness and suspicion, found the little lad a most pleasant companion, eager to learn all he could tell him of the strange and wonderful sights passing around him, anxious, too, to understand his little sister's strange words about the king and the bishops.

The boy's mind was opening and ripening,

but Harry Vane wondered how far it would
be well for him to know of the strife that
was continually growing in Church and State,
and had already created the New England to
which they were sailing, and which they would
probably find very different from the dear
home-country they were leaving far behind.

At length he decided to tell the lad something of the great struggle that was now con-
vulsing not only England but the whole Continent of Europe; for the German war was still
raging, and Rupert's father was fighting with
sword and battle-ax for freedom and liberty of
conscience, as Pym and Hampden had fought
by protests and remonstrances many a like
battle in the English Parliament; still the
struggle was going on — the war of right
against might — in which all who loved the
truth *must* engage, if they would win the truth
for themselves.

Many an hour did they sit on the deck of
the little vessel, wrapped closely in their warm
frieze coats, for it was cold weather now, talking of the grand battle that was going on in
the world—the battle that Luther had begun
and Calvin carried on as far as he was able,
but which the powers of darkness seemed to
have determined should be carried no farther.

Henceforth men's minds were to be bound in the fetters of the past; there was to be no more growth. God himself was to stand aside and make no further revelations to man, and men, for their part, were to shrink from the thought that God had not yet given them all he had to give, or, at the peril of losing their souls, were to receive any further manifestations of truth from him.

Not in the very words I have written· did Harry Vane talk to the lad, thrown upon him for companionship; but they contain the gist and kernel of many conversations, and embodied the broad living principle that ruled Vane's own life and belief, and which he now tried to make Rupert Saxby understand. He did understand it as far as his mind was able to receive it, and, what was of infinitely more value, he believed in his teacher, for he saw, day by day and hour by hour, that he exemplified his teaching in his own Christ-like life, so large in its charity for others, so strict and blameless in the regulation of his own; and, although no word was said of the sacrifices he had made for conscience' sake, Rupert Saxby knew that these were many, and he wondered how the world could be wicked with two such men in it as Master Hampden and Master Harry Vane.

CHAPTER XIX.

NEW BOSTON.

HOW eagerly our travelers looked out for the shores of New England our readers can well imagine. The colony had grown rapidly, for there were now sixteen towns in all clustered round Boston, which was one of the earliest formed, and named in loving remembrance of the English port from which they had embarked for Holland.

Rupert Saxby was eager to know what this New England was like; but Master Vane could only shake his head and tell the boy he would probably find many things different from what they were in the old country, while at the same time he tried to prepare his own mind for some disappointment—some shock, perhaps, to all his preconceived notions of what this new country would be like.

At length the little timber-built fort, with its two or three mounted guns, commanding the harbor, rose upon their view, and no sooner was it known that a ship from England was in the offing than the colonists crowded the shores, eager to welcome the strangers, many hoping to find friends among them.

Harry Vane was glad he had donned a homely frieze cloak and doublet, for satin and velvet would look sadly out of place among these soberly dressed people, although it was evident many of them wore their holiday dress in honor of the arrival of friends.

And then the town! Why, it seemed as though the wilderness and civilization had met in a death-struggle; but it was hard to say which would conquer yet. Little, strongly built log-huts, set down in the midst of gardens and fields, that looked as though they were now only half reclaimed from the forest, were the best mansions that Boston could boast; and into one of these Harry was taken, for he bore letters of introduction to friends of Pym and Hampden—learned and accomplished gentlemen, who had left estates and mansions in England for liberty of conscience.

His host was not at home, but at work in some distant fields, his wife said; but she received Harry Vane with all the grace and courtesy of a high-born English lady, that seemed only the more striking from the humble surroundings. Her visitor could hardly speak for a minute or two, so striking was the contrast—the rough, unplaned logs that formed the cottage walls, the low door-way, the wide kitchen fire-place opposite the rough home-made settles, with one or two handsome oak chests that occupied the place of honor just under the book-shelves close to the window.

Rupert Saxby looked round too, and felt something like boyish disgust at the rude, homely surroundings. This was evidently kitchen, dining-room, library, and visitors' parlor all in one, and he had for the last few years enjoyed the abundance and refinement of Master Hampden's luxurious home, and felt the contrast to be painful indeed.

Presently the master of the house came in, hastened in his return by the messenger sent for him. He was a tall, stately, grave-looking man, with a broad, massive brow, that contrasted almost as strongly with his soiled hands and earth-stained clothes as his wife's stately courtesy did with the log-cabin in which they lived.

Master Vane was welcomed to the colony and all the host's house would afford before the letter was read informing him who his visitor was, and how highly Master Pym esteemed him ; but when he had read this his face beamed with delight, and he hastened to lay aside the leather jerkin he wore, and put on more suitable attire, although it was only of homely frieze, such as had shocked Dame Meredith's refined sense of what was becoming for her nephew. .

While their host was changing his dress in a little lean-to, that formed their only dressing-room, and their hostess was busy in preparing them a meal, Harry Vane told Rupert that his friend was one of the most learned men of the age, and had been offered the chair of the Professor of Rhetoric at Cambridge to induce him to stay there. They looked at the books in the hanging shelves—books in several languages, learned treatises, which none but the most cultivated minds could understand and appreciate. Rupert had seen companion volumes in Master Hampden's library at home: but here—was ever any thing so incongruous as this log-cabin and this little library on its walls?

Suddenly Master Vane turned to the lad and said: "God is going to make a great and mighty nation here, I trow, and he has set worthy men to be the fathers and founders of it. Look you, lad; these are no sickly bookworms who must die inside their college walls, but men made in God's own image, who can work with their hands as well as their brains, and are not afraid or ashamed to do it."

In a short time the table had been spread for the meal, and now came another contrast. Silver drinking-cups, exquisitely chased and beautified, stood beside wooden platters, and the finest table linen covered the rough table. But if the lady of the house was her own cook, as well as chamber-maid and dairy-maid, no fault could be found with the sweet wholesome bread and delicate golden butter and honey, or the tasty little dishes that had been got ready almost by magic, and cooked in the room where they were eaten.

Such a merry meal as that was! the host asking after old friends in England, and telling who had joined them in the New England, and the hostess waiting upon them with the gentle grace of Dame Hampden herself, in spite of her homely surroundings.

"And so this little lad is another Saxby, come out to help his grandparents with the new Saxby they are making here," said their host.

"Is my grandfather's place called Saxby?" Rupert ventured to ask.

"Yes, my lad, it is; and a goodly place it is, or will be; and if thy other uncle and thy father could but come over here, the old man's heart would be at rest.   He clung steadfastly to the old Saxby, the home of his forefathers, but God has led him to a goodly heritage here, and he hath but one desire now, to be rid of the old place, lest it rob him of his children."

The meal was over, and the host proposed that they should call upon their minister, Master John Cotton.   He was formerly rector of St. Botolph's, Boston, for nearly twenty years, but the growth of despotism in the Church under Laud, and its subservience to the State, had at last compelled him to resign his living and seek a refuge among his Puritan friends in the new Boston they had founded.   As they passed the little wattled church, less pretentious than many a gentleman's barn in the old country, Harry Vane and his friend stopped to look at it.

" Master Cotton must surely feel the difference between this and his old church," said Harry Vane; "for the church of Boston is more like a cathedral than any other in England."

" Yes, yes, 'tis a grand building, Master Vane, and I am not of those who would despise such, for I hold that God should have of our best; but still Master Cotton has in this little wattled church what he had not at last

in yonder stone temple—liberty to teach the
whole doctrine of God; and that is dearer to
such a man than splendid churches and costly
living. But here comes worthy Master Cotton
himself, and I can see my boys and girls just
beyond him, too."

The young folks passed the minister, but not
unrecognized. Each bowed in lowly reverence
before this honored servant of God; the boys
doffing their caps and the girls dropping a
courtsey as they wished him good day. They
stopped before their father, paying him the
same deference, and glancing shyly at the
stranger as they passed. They were just returning from school, and their father bade
them hasten home, as their mother wanted
John to fetch her water from the well and
Molly to scour the platters.

"Our young ones must all be useful here,"
he remarked to Harry Vane.

"And God's blessing will always be with
them while they are," said the minister, who
overheard the remark. "And who have we
here?" he said, extending his hand to Harry
Vane. "Another friend from the dear home-
land, I trow."

"This is Master Vane, whose father is of
the king's household," said his host.

"Ah, a court gallant; and what may bring such fine birds among us?" said the old minister, a little doubtfully.

"Nay, nay, good Master Cotton, I am no court gallant, and have grievously offended my father and the king thereby," said Harry Vane, while his host hastened to say how warmly he had been commended by Master Pym, in his letter of introduction. "I was even now bringing to you the letter and my visitor," he added, as they paused at the minister's garden gate.

"Come in, come in," said Master Cotton, leading the way into a little log-cabin, no more pretentious-looking than the rest. Next to the governor, Master Cotton considered himself the chief protector of the little colony, and he was by no means disposed to have fine court gallants, fresh from the frivolous life of Whitehall, going about among his flock, leading the young ones astray, and teaching them all sorts of idle vanities, if not worse; and so, after inviting his visitors to be seated, he sat down himself and prepared to examine Harry Vane, both by question and the study of his face.

Few young men could have passed such an ordeal without losing their temper, but Harry

17

Vane understood the old man's motive, and was quite willing that he should assure himself at once that he was not a wolf in sheep's clothing, which he evidently feared.

When it was over, Master Cotton rose and grasped the hand of Vane, saying, "Welcome to our colony, and may your stay among us be for many years, an the Lord will."

"It must be seen first whether I can be of service to you, " said Vane.

"Well, well, there is little doubt of the service, I trow; for we are glad of any who can help us with hands or brains. And now, having told me so much about yourself and your life, it is meet I should tell you how I came to be in this place, after serving the Lord twenty years in the dear old Boston of the home-land."

"Nay, sir, I doubt not it was for conscience' sake," said Harry.

"But conscience and reason should go together, young man; and think not because a few good men have come here they are all fools or all bad that stay behind. But I had been watching the course of the Church of England for more than twenty years, and during all that time she was growing more and more corrupt. The Reformation had been

cut short before its work was done. It went
on, see you, in the hearts and minds of the
people, but stopped short in the Church. It
was not perceived at first, but in proportion
to what she at last felt to be the growing dis-
taste in which her corruptions were held by
the people did she seek support from the
crown by making her sacred functions subservient to its arbitrary purposes. There is
no country, except Rome itself, where an alli-
ance with the State has led churchmen into
such shameless servility as England; until,
at last, my Lord of Canterbury, knowing the
king wants to raise an illegal loan, does but
send letters throughout the kingdom, and
forthwith every pulpit is used to teach the
doctrine that if the king's right to do this is
denied or questioned it is at the peril of his
soul who shall dare to do it; and I, John Cotton, as a true Englishman and honest man,
could but refuse to preach this."

" I would to God that many others would
do likewise. But 'tis well that we have not
the keeping of other men's consciences, and
that we are bidden to 'judge not,' " added
Harry Vane.

He had taken Master Cotton's heart by
storm as well as his host's, and it was with

some difficulty that he could get away from Boston until other visits had been paid ; but he was anxious to take Rupert Saxby to his grandparents with as little delay as possible, and so preparations for the thirty miles' journey to Ipswich was commenced at once.

Thirty miles' journey through forest clearings, in a bullock wagon, was not a rapid mode of traveling, and so Rupert did not reach Saxby until he had been nearly a week in the colony, and somewhat used to the strange condition of things he saw around him. The strangeness had worn off a little, and he was better able to appreciate the substantial comfort of his grandfather's log-house, although it did lack many of the comforts and luxuries to which he had been accustomed at Hampden.

He was received with almost rapturous delight by Dame Saxby as well as her husband, and even his likeness to his French mother was forgiven and forgotten when he said, " I am so glad you have called this nice new place Saxby."

" He is the same, the very same, boy that we spoke to at Southampton," said Dame Saxby, looking him over critically.

" I do not remember you, madam," said Rupert.

" Perhaps not, and I did not know that I should remember you; for it was the little wench I noticed most. Where is she? Where is your sister?" suddenly asked the dame.

" She is in England, madam," said Rupert; and then Harry Vane hastened to explain how fond his aunt had grown of the little girl, and how unwilling to part with her to any but her own father, and how impossible it was for him to bring her without a maid-servant.

" Dear heart! if I had only known, I would have come myself to fetch the little wench," said her grandmother, almost crying with disappointment; for she had made up her mind that the children would come together when they did come.

It was needless to ask if the old couple were happy in their wilderness home. Master Saxby looked ten years younger than he did when he left England, although he had been working harder than ever he did in his life before. But, as he explained to Harry Vane, his heart was at rest now. He was never in fear of being driven from his home or harassed by fines and imprisonment if he ventured to cross its threshold. They had long walks and talks together, Harry Vane learning much of the polity and self-government of the colony; how the governor was assisted by a council of assessors; how all paid a tax in money or the produce of their farms for the making of roads and such other public works as were necessary for the general comfort and safety of all; how the lands were bought of the Indians and fairly paid for, and how anxious the colonists were to keep up their friendly relations with all the tribes of the country, if possible.

Saxby was at the outermost fringe of civilization, reclaimed from the primeval forest, and so they often saw some of the red-skins, but they had had little trouble with them beyond a few fights at first, and Master Saxby was now warmly interested in a question that had lately been mooted among them by Master Eliot, the minister of Roxbury, who thought it was the duty of Christian people to try and convert the heathen. This doctrine was too new and strange to win general acceptance; some good souls looking upon the project as nothing less than presumption. But Harry Vane did not look upon it in this light, and entered so warmly into the scheme that Master Saxby declared he would go back with him to Roxbury and introduce him to Master John Eliot.

CHAPTER XX.

GOVERNOR VANE.

A WEEK or two was spent at Saxby and visiting the neighboring town of Ipswich, during which time Master Vane made many friends for himself, and gained a few for Master Eliot's project for teaching the Indians the truths of the gospel as well as the arts of civilization. He obtained promises of material help, too, for this first apostle to the Indians; for Harry Vane had the rare gift of inspiring others with enthusiasm—a gift which brought him many friends, but often as many foes. At present, however, he had none but friends among the colonists, who were as much charmed by Harry Vane's pleasant manner as by the fact of his having so resolutely turned his back upon the world, and chosen that " better part " which led him to cast in his lot with these few despised Puritans, when he might be enjoying every court favor. Dame Saxby was sorry to part with her guest, but he promised to visit them again, and, what was even better, send them a parcel of books

and copies of Butler's first newspaper, which
would tell them all about the German war.
Master Saxby could bring these back with him
from Boston when his work as an assessor was
over.   The laws of that period were rather
Draco-like, and offenses singled out with a mi-
nuteness that must have given magistrates
some work to do even in such a small and well-
ordered community.   Witchcraft, perjury, and
blasphemy were made capital offenses, and
children were also punished with death for
cursing or striking their parents.   All who
were detected either in lying, drunkenness, or
dancing were to be publicly whipped.   Doubtless these severe punishments had a deterrent
effect upon a few when they first came to the
colony—young men who came with parents
and friends—but the moral atmosphere of the
whole community was far more effective than
any laws that could be enacted, however severe.   Harry Vane paid a visit to Master Eliot
at Roxbury, and then took up his residence
at Boston.

When he had been here little more than a
year the colonists showed their estimation of
him by choosing him for governor at the an-
nual election.   This was in the year 1636, when
Harry Vane was little more than twenty-four

years of age. The rejoicings in which the
people indulged upon that occasion called for
some tact and management on the part of the
new governor, such as one rarely sees in so
young a man. There were fifteen large vessels in port, which fired a salute to the new
governor; and this calling the attention of the
inhabitants to their presence, a deputation
waited upon Vane, stating that such a large
force of foreign vessels was in itself a disagreeable circumstance in the condition of a feeble
settlement. Vane saw the justice of it at once,
and even more than had been represented, for
there was no doubt that the influence of the
habits of the men of these ships could not be
other than injurious to the morals and social
condition of the inhabitants of the town. But
how to alter this without giving offense to the
captains of the vessels, and thus injuring the
commerce of the growing little colony, was a
matter not so easily settled.

At length the new governor invited all the
captains of the vessels to dine with him, and
after dinner laid the difficulty before them,
when it was discussed in the most friendly
manner on both sides. The adjustment of it
which Master Vane proposed was readily
agreed to, which was that all inward bound

vessels should anchor below the fort, and wait for the governor's pass before coming up to the town, and, last but not least, that the crews should never be allowed on shore after sunset.

A little later there was another and even more delicate matter to settle between the colonists and some captains about hoisting the English flag, where Vane's tact saved them not only from offending the touchy seamen, but, what was of far more importance just now, from giving any shadow of offense to the home government. What difficulties this tact of the young governor saved the struggling colony they, doubtless, never knew, though they did know later—what private friends had, doubtless, informed Vane of at the time—that the home government was growing jealous of the rising colony; and this same year the whole of it was sold in Westminster Hall over the heads of the inhabitants, and in direct violation of the patent granted by James to the original settlers who went over in the "Mayflower." It is true no action was taken upon this sale, but had the colonists given the slightest offense, doubtless advantage would have been taken of this, and Vane, who knew the tempers of both parties, foresaw it.

About the same time another difficult question came to the front, which the aristocratic young governor doubtless had no inconsiderable share in deciding, though it was against his own class in society. Lord Say and Lord Brooke had always been good friends to the colonists, helping them most materially, and at this time they sent to propose coming to the colony to settle, with a few other gentlemen. But the proposal was burdened with conditions. The new-comers were to form an upper and distinct class; their heirs and successors were always to be gentlemen. Then the colony was to be governed by two houses of legislature; the first to consist of this hereditary peerage, answering to the English House of Lords, and from among these alone the governor was to be chosen; the lower house to consist of freeholders, as representatives of the whole people. Doubtless the coming of such noblemen would bring many present advantages to the colonists, but these men had not forsaken all things for any temporal advantage, however great, and they felt, as doubtless their young governor foresaw, that they would be bartering their dear-bought liberty for a very questionable gain, and a courteous but decided refusal was sent to the two noblemen.

A few months after his election as governor letters arrived from England pressing him to return at once, and he was disposed to do so, on account of a religious controversy that had arisen, and which threatened to separate dearest friends in its fierceness.

The keen intellectual life of Boston, even when she could only boast of log-cabins and turf-thatched churches, made her society peculiarly liable to this form of discussion; and the arrival of an accomplished English lady, Mrs. Anne Hutchinson, set the whole colony together by the ears, and soon brought upon herself and young Governor Vane the charge of heresy. As godly Master Cotton, however, was himself among the heretics, we may be sure the heresy was not of a very strong type, and consisted for the most part in Harry Vane's old claim of liberty of conscience for all. Our Puritan forefathers did not understand liberty after the Vane type. They claimed that men should have liberty to think as *they* did, but they must go no further; and doubtless it was very annoying to Master Wilson and other learned divines to have their long sermons pulled to pieces and criticised by a clever woman like Dame Hutchinson, in the presence of half the matrons of the city.

It was the custom for the members of the
Church to meet each week to talk over and
impress upon their minds the discourses of
the previous Sunday; and Dame Hutchinson, following out this custom, soon instituted
similar meetings for women. So attractive
and interesting were these prayer-meetings
that nearly all the ladies in the place attended
them.

The clergy of the colony were startled at
first, and then grew jealous of the free inquiry
that was encouraged at these meetings, and
of the influence the new-comer was gaining
over the minds of their flocks. She, with a lack
of wisdom and Christian charity, retaliated
by criticising the previous Sunday's sermon,
or circulating imputations against their learning and the soundness of the doctrine they
preached.

This was not to be borne. She herself was
a heretic, and must be handed over for punishment due to heresy. At this point Governor
Vane interfered to protect Dame Hutchinson
from her enemies, and the controversy grew
more fierce and bitter from that time. The
truth seems to be that both Harry Vane and
Dame Hutchinson were a little ahead of the
age in which they lived; and what we should

call a large-hearted Christian charity was by our stricter forefathers branded as laxity in doctrine and perilous heresy.

This, at last, drove Master Vane from the land of his adoption, and he returned to England in the autumn of 1637.

But if New England was in a state of ferment over a religious difficulty, old England was no less disturbed by the famous trial that had just taken place between Master Hampden and the king over the famous ship-money business. This was the king's last mode of increasing the revenue; but, ostensibly for the purpose of maintaining a fleet, it was at first imposed on sea-ports only, but soon extended to inland towns, and, as one of the famous lawyers of the day characterized it, was, in fact, "a spring and magazine that should have no bottom, and for an everlasting supply on all occasions."

People grumbled, but had paid this tax, illegal as it was deemed to be; but Master Hampden refused, and tested the case as a point of law. The decision had been against him through the servility of time-serving judges, but there had been so great difference in their various judgments that the whole trial was a severe blow to the State.

But if there was little political freedom, there was less for those who dared to differ in religious matters. A pitiable scene had been enacted this summer in front of Westminster Hall, by order of the Star-chamber. A doctor, minister, and lawyer, three learned men and worthy citizens, had been publicly whipped, their noses slit, their ears cut off, and, thus maimed, had been branded in the cheek, and imprisoned for life. The minister's offense was writing a book entitled "Zion's Plea against Prelacy," and the other two had given voice to the popular discontent against the illegal acts of the king and corruptions of the court.

So if Master Vane found it difficult to live peaceably in New England, he was not likely to find life a bed of roses in his old home; for Laud had carried things with a high hand since he had been Archbishop of Canterbury, and the king under his persuasion had attempted to force episcopacy upon his Scottish subjects.

When Harry Vane reached his father's house in the Strand, the first result of this attempt was being warmly discussed in many an English household, and nowhere with greater warmth or greater pity than between Dame

Meredith and her adopted daughter, Winifred
Saxby. How they pitied those foolish, igno-
rant Scotch people, who could see no beauty
in priestly vestments and ecclesiastical orna-
ments, and even resisted the introduction of a
prayer-book, preferring their own bald service
to any thing the English Church could give
them in exchange! But who shall picture the
horror and indignation of Winifred when the
news reached her of what had taken place
in Edinburgh that July Sunday, when Jenny
Geddes had thrown her stool at the bishop's
head? It had been the signal for hisses and
groans, and cries of "A pope! a pope! Down
with the priest of Baal!" and what had been
begun as a most impressive and awe-inspiring
service ended in a riot and a general flight of
the clergy.

"Is not the sin of this Scotch woman unpardonable?" asked Winifred, with a little
shiver. She was sitting at the window, looking
through the tiny lozenge-shaped eye-holes of
glass at the river, with its burden of boats and
barges, and one of these was being moored to
their own private steps at the bottom of the
garden.

"Somebody is coming here, madam," she
remarked.

"I have told Dorothy I do not wish to be disturbed to-day," said Dame Meredith.

She had only reached London the day before, and news of this Scotch business had not penetrated to the quiet of Hadlow, and so this and various other items almost as painful and disturbing had met her all at once in London. Poor Dame Meredith, who thought the Church of England perfect, or at least growing every day more perfect under Archbishop Laud's direction, had had high hopes for this Scotch episcopacy movement; and how people could willfully resist what was intended for their good she was at a loss to understand.

"If people would only be quiet, and let the king and archbishop have their own way, how much better it would be for them!" she said, following out her own thoughts rather than answering Winny's question.

"How is it, madam, that people dare to disobey God's anointed?" asked the girl.

"Because they do not understand, or will not believe, that all that is done is for their good. If they could once believe this, I feel sure they would not resist as they do, and—"

But here the talk was interrupted by the entrance of Dorothy, who, with a lurking smile, but all-becoming gravity, announced,

18

"The Governor of Massachusetts." If she had announced a Sachem of the Pequot Indians, Dame Meredith could not have looked more astonished than she did as she said, "I do not receive strangers to-day, and this foreigner must want my Cousin Vane."

"So you decline to receive me, aunt?" said Harry Vane, laughing, as he slipped from behind the old waiting woman.

"Harry, Harry! what! at your school-boy tricks still? I wonder how often you have played that joke upon us?" said Dame Meredith, in a tremor of delight, and yet turning pale at this sudden apparition of her beloved nephew.

In a moment Harry saw that his aunt was changed. The two or three years that seemed as nothing to him, now he was back in the old room, had aged her wonderfully. Perhaps it was the first time it had ever come upon him that she was growing old, but it came with marvelous distinctness now, and the next thought was about Winifred, and what would become of her in case of her guardian's death.

He put them from him now, but they had found a lodgment in his mind, and his talk this first day took some color from the hidden thought; for he suddenly remembered how anti-Puritan this girl's education had of necessity been, and how painful her lot might be when she joined her own friends, whose opinions differed so widely from those in which she had been reared.

" The Governor of Massachusetts!" repeated Dame Meredith. " Methinks you might have chosen a more honorable title, and one that smacks less of rebellion against his majesty," said the lady.

" Dorothy made a slight mistake. I said the late Governor of Massachusetts. Did you not hear of the honor the good folks yonder had conferred upon me ? "

" Honor ! " repeated the lady with a very questionable sniff. " We heard some such idle gossip, but thought it well to forget it again, and I mean to forget that and every other disagreeable thing now you have come home to us. You have seen your father, Harry ? "

" Yes, and he is pleased to say he is glad to have me back," replied the young man.

" Did he tell you the news ? " asked his aunt.

" I have heard too much news. That about Prynne and Bostwick is shameful."

" Yes, yes, I think the Star-chamber is a

little too hard sometimes," admitted Dame Meredith, "but it was not that I meant, but this Scotch business that is so sorely troubling the king and archbishop just now;" and Dame Meredith told the story of the throwing of Jenny Geddes' stool, and the riot that followed.

Almost unconsciously Winny was drawn into taking part in the discussion that followed, and Harry Vane questioned and talked to her, growing each moment more painfully convinced of the depth and earnestness of her religious opinions, and how, like his aunt, to her mind the questioning the right of king or bishop to do any thing they pleased was like doubting God himself.

CHAPTER XXI.

PERPLEXITIES.

SUMMER sunshine was again flooding the pleasant gardens of Dame Meredith's mansion at Hadlow, which she rarely left now. The change which Harry Vane had noticed some years before had now become apparent to every body—the visits to London had grown more infrequent, and, unwilling as Dame Meredith was to admit it, her growing infirmities compelled her to keep almost entirely to her own room.

The younger Vanes often came to visit her and bring her the news of what was going on in the world ; for the old lady took as keen an interest in what was going forward as ever she did ; but lately Winny had taken upon herself to sift this news, begging the young Vanes to keep back any thing that would cause her dear old friend the least disquiet.

These were disquieting times, and the self-imposed censorship often made Winny look grave and anxious beyond her years. She was eighteen now—a tall, stately, dignified girl, as she was compelled to be, having taken the direction of Dame Meredith's household upon her young shoulders, and behaving in all things as a daughter to the friend who had sheltered her in her helplessness. Not that she felt herself forsaken by her own kindred; sometimes she almost wished she had been, for she knew all too well now the wide difference that existed between them; but how a noble, brave-hearted soldier, like her father, who had left his country and spent the best years of his life fighting for King Charles' sister, could at the same time sympathize with such men as Pym and Hampden, was a puzzle Winny could not understand. Clearly he must be mistaken. In the far-off Germany he could not understand the battle that was being waged against the king by these obstinate, misguided men; and surely their last act—the impious daring they had been guilty of in arresting and imprisoning Archbishop Laud— would convince him how utterly unworthy they were of his regard.

This imprisonment of the archbishop was a dread weight upon poor Winny. Hitherto she had carefully guarded the secret from Dame Meredith, for she feared to tell her lest the blow should lay her utterly prostrate.

She knew the horror that had seized her when she heard of the awful crime the Parliament had committed in laying its ruthless hands upon the sacred person of the archbishop. What they would not dare to do now Winny was at a loss to know—perhaps imprison the king himself, if ever they had the power; and there was no telling what might happen, since they had come to open warfare. Strange to say, this open warfare between the king and his Parliament affected Winny far less than the imprisonment of the archbishop. Several battles had been fought during the last nine months, Prince Rupert, the king's nephew, leading the royalist army, and often fighting against old friends, who had learned all the tactics of war in fighting for his father and mother and the Palatinate, which represented the Protestant cause of Europe. But battles even between Englishmen, and fought on English ground, were nothing in Winny's mind as compared with the assault made on God's Church in the person of the archbishop. So when young Mistress Vane came and whispered, "Another battle has been fought," Winny said, "Will it make them release the archbishop, think you?"

"Nay, nay, I fear not, for our enemies are

stubborn. But who, think you, has been killed in this battle? 'Twas fought at Chalgrove field, not far from Saxby, my brother tells us."

For a moment Winny shook her head, and then, with a touch of anxiety in her tone, she said,

"Not Master Hampden, I hope!"

Her companion looked at her in surprise.

"Why should you feel sorry for the death of that rebel?" she said. "You are almost as bad as Harry, and I never saw him so moved as when the messenger blurted out the news, forgetting he was almost a rebel himself."

The younger Vanes rarely admitted so much as this as to their brother's opinions, for he was a great puzzle to them, as he was to many others.

"But why should you be sorry, Winny?" asked her companion again.

"Because my father will be so sorry and disappointed. He is coming home, you know, in a few weeks, and in his last letter he said half the joy of his home-coming would be in seeing his old friend, Master John Hampden."

"Your father is coming back. Will he join this rebel army, think you?"

"My father join the rebels, who have seized the archbishop!" exclaimed Winny with something like scorn.

"You forget he is a soldier, and may—"

"Hush, hush!" interrupted Winny, holding up her hands as if to ward off a threatened blow.

"There, hush, dear; I did not mean to hurt you. I know what you are feeling; for we all feel the same about our poor misguided brother. Is he not doing all he can to help Oliver Cromwell and Lord Fairfax, if he is not actually fighting himself, and—and worse even than that, Winny? I do not mind telling you, because you, too, have friends among these crop-eared roundheads, and can feel for us. Harry's journey to Scotland, by and by, is to make a solemn league and covenant, as they call it, with the Scotch to help each other in the reformation of religion and the extirpation of popery and prelacy; so that there is little hope of seeing the archbishop released yet, I fear."

The mention of the archbishop brought back to Winny's mind the fear that had been uppermost for some days, lest Dame Meredith should hear this suddenly and without preparation.

"Would it not be better, think you, to tell her, since there is so little hope of his release?" said Winny. "We have kept this secret so long; but the tale your father told her, about the archbishop's living in strict retirement, she is beginning to doubt, I fear, for she has questioned me several times of late."

"Poor Winny! how can I tell you what we have all begun to fear at home? You know the archbishop's trial is to take place soon."

"Yes, yes; how dare they presume to judge one whom God alone has the right to bring to judgment?" exclaimed Winny.

"But they have determined to do it, and they will not— My father fears the trial will go against Laud," young Mistress Vane hastened to add.

"And if it should, what then?—what could they do?" asked Winny.

"What they did to Lord Stafford a little while ago," said her friend scarcely above her breath.

Winny started away in horror-stricken fright. "They would never do that," she said. "They would never stain their hands with his sacred blood."

"There is no telling what they may do; for

you see the hedge of sacred ordinance, that to us would be his strongest safeguard, has no existence for them. He is no more than an ordinary man to these roundheads, you must remember."

" But even if it be so, what can they accuse him of worthy of death? He has led a pure life, and—"

" No one has a word to say against his personal character, but he is to be charged with trying to subvert liberty and religion, and practicing cruelty and oppression through the courts of Star-chamber and High-commission."

Winny shook her head. " He will not be the first martyr," she said ; " but, still, I hope his life may be spared, that when these troubles are over he may proceed with his work for the Church. How sorely it would grieve him could he know how his work has already been undone—how the churches have been stripped and the altars removed ! "

" Yes, indeed ; it is a mercy for dear aunt that she cannot go to church now, to see how bare it is once more," said young Mistress Vane.

" But, do you know, she has begun to talk of going again, now that the warm weather

has come?   She says it is all very well to
spend the hours we are at church in her oratory, but it is not like worshiping God in the
great congregation, and she cannot let such
small ailments as hers interfere with what is
a positive duty."

"Poor, dear aunt! I wish we could spare
her this pain, Winny; but if she has set her
mind upon this, she must be told the truth
about the archbishop."

"And I have to tell her that my father is
coming home at last, and that I know she has
always dreaded; for we cannot tell what he
may wish me to do."

"O Winny, you will never leave her?" said
her companion quickly.

"I hope not, dear—I will not if I can help
it; but I know it has always been my father's
wish that when he came home I should go
with him wherever he might decide to live,
and it is most likely that he will want to go
to this New England."

"Where they are all crop-eared roundheads
and drawling Precisians! O, my poor Winny,
what a dreadful fate!"

"Do not laugh at me," said Winny, almost
ready to cry. "Every thing seems in such a
dreadful tangle for every body. How can we

know what to do, or even what to pray for? If things were only a little different—if there were no good men on the wrong side ; but there is Master Vane, and I feel sure, from all I have heard, Master Hampden was as good, and—"

"Yes, my father says there is less possibility than ever of a reconciliation between the king and Parliament now John Hampden has gone. He had always hoped that Hampden and Lord Falkland might have made peace between them ; for, although he cannot agree with Harry, he says he chose for his friends the best men in the country."

"Yes, that is where it is so hard, that so many good men are on the wrong side, and forced to do such evil deeds."

The two young ladies had wandered round the garden and back to the house, and as they reached the door old Dorothy came to tell them Dr. Andrew Fuller had just arrived. He had been spending some time with the king at Oxford, where the rival Parliament was sitting and the court had taken up its abode.

He was a tall, stately man, but his blue eyes seemed to brim over with mirthfulness ; yet he was as pious, and ruled his life with as much strictness, as any Puritan, although he was a stanch royalist and a great friend of Dame Meredith, whom he had come some miles out of his way to visit. He, understanding and appreciating the piety and earnestness of such men as Harry Vane, and Pym, and Hampden, had tried to make peace between the contending parties a few weeks before; but the rebels, though they listened to his sermon courteously enough—as he told the young ladies—would have made him a rebel, too, if they could, so he had left London to try what he could do among the cavaliers at Oxford. But his sermons were less appreciated by the rollicking soldiers and court gallants than by their enemies; still he had great hopes of Lord Falkland being able to do something, if the king would only restrain such men as Prince Rupert from going too far.

"It is such a pity that all good men do not range themselves on the side of the king!" said Winny, when she had given orders for refreshments to be brought into the cedar parlor, and heard from old Dorothy that Dame Meredith was taking her midday nap.

"Aye, my wenches, it is a sore puzzle to me sometimes; but I trow God can see through the mists and tangles of this life, and, though the storm may be fierce, the ark of his Church will outride the roughest billows."

"You think the Church is safe, although the archbishop is in prison?" said Winny, who, like many another timid soul, just now thought the safety of the Church was ·bound up in Archbishop Laud.

"Yes, yes, God is not going to forsake his Church, although it may be for our sins we shall be sorely tried; and lest we trust too much in ordinances, some of these may be removed, that we may cleave the closer to God himself."

"I wish I could believe this always," sighed Winny.

"It is not thy faith, but God's faithfulness, you must rely upon," said Dr. Fuller; and at this moment Dorothy came to say that her mistress was awake, and would be glad to see her visitor when he had rested and refreshed himself.

His frugal meal was soon made, for he was one of the most abstemious of men; but before he went to Dame Meredith Winny contrived to explain to him the difficulty she was in through the little deceit that had been practiced upon her aunt concerning the archbishop's imprisonment.

The good man shook his head disapprovingly. "Crooked ways are sure to land us in difficulties," he said; but he undertook to break the painful news to his old friend, and also hint at some of the changes that had already been effected in the Church and ritual—how it had been robbed of what Dame Meredith called "the beauty of holiness," for the more simple form of worship that had prevailed years before.

It was arranged that Dr. Fuller should spend a few days at Hadlow, for which Winny was most thankful afterward, for the very day of his arrival she was summoned to see a tall bronzed stranger, who refused to give his name at first, asking only for Mistress Winifred Saxby, whom she supposed must be another messenger from her father—another veteran from the German war, come to fight in the rebel army.

He did not make himself known for some time, hoping that some recollection lingered in Winny's mind of her father; but he forgot the lapse of time, and almost failed himself to recognize in the stately young lady, who seemed so perfectly at ease in this luxurious home, the little, curly-haired darling, who had met him with gleeful shouts of joy whenever the exigencies of the war allowed him to return for a few days to his home.

But at last he made himself known, and Winny was locked in the arms of the father she had so often tried to picture to herself. The reality did not disappoint her. She looked up through the mist of tears that had gathered in her eyes with a glow of pride at the bronzed, worn face that had faced so many battles, and carried almost a charmed life through the dangers and vicissitudes of this long German war. It was a brave, noble face, telling of calm self-surrender and self-conquest, that stamped it as the brow of a victor, whose word none would gainsay or doubt. Winny was content with her father, and in this their first meeting her heart went out to him, and she felt willing at once that he should decide as to her future.

It was with this thought in her mind that she said, " You will not ask me to leave Dame Meredith yet, father? she is ill; she cannot live many years, and it will break her heart to lose me just now when so many sad things are happening."

" My dear, you owe her the duty of a daughter, and how could I grudge your loving service to one who has been as a mother indeed to you!"

19

"Then, you will not ask me to go with you to New England yet."

"To New England, my wench? I am not going to New England—at least, not yet. Rupert is coming over here—I expect him in a few weeks—for old England needs the help of all her sons just now."

For a moment Winny forgot the difference in their opinions, and stood with clasped hands and radiant face. "I am so glad," she said; "so glad you have come to help the king before the rebels have gained any decisive victory."

"My dear, the king has no more loyal subjects in this realm than those brave gentlemen whom you call rebels. I am come to serve under Colonel Cromwell, who needs a better army than tapsters and 'prentice lads."

Winny's hands dropped at her side, and she fell back a pace or two, as though she had been struck a deadly blow. "O, my father," she gasped, "I thought if you only came to England, and heard about the archbishop being in prison, and all about the quarrel, you would surely help the king and try to save our English Church from those who would destroy it."

"I do know all about the quarrel, Winny. It began before you were born, before I left England, and has been slowly growing through

Father and Daugnter.

all these years. The people have been robbed of their rights and liberty, even their liberty to serve God according to their own conscience. It was this that drove your grandsire, and thousands like him, away from their father-land, and now, at last, the yoke has grown too heavy to be longer borne. We must break it or die. Good-night, Winny; I will come again to-morrow and see Dame Meredith."

CHAPTER XXII.

CONCLUSION.

IT would be hard to describe poor Winny's feelings after her father left her. Somehow she had allowed herself to hope that when he came home he would see at once how mistaken he had been, and withdraw the sympathy he had hitherto felt for these Puritans, who wanted the world turned upside down for their convenience. Now these half-formed hopes were all rudely shattered, for it was plain that her father had come home on purpose to serve in the rebel army, and it might be that he would get killed without a moment granted for repentance, or time to understand the awful mistake he had been under.

This was a terrible thought to Winny. She had often prayed for Jenny Geddes, that God would pardon her for throwing her stool at the bishop that summer Sunday morning, almost fearing the sin might be unpardonable; but how much greater was her father's, in raising his hand against the king's sacred majesty in open rebellion! She and Dame Meredith had talked over the news concerning Hampden, and, hearing a rumor that though mortally wounded he was not dead, they had prayed that God would grant him the gift of repentance in those last days of his life, that his sun might not go down in utter darkness. Now the same prayer would be offered for her father, but it afforded poor comfort to Winny just now.

The news of Master Saxby's return was broken to Dame Meredith the next day, but, at the same time, Winny assured her that he had no wish to take her away at present.

"He will not have to wait long for you, my Winny," said the old lady, stroking the girl's shining hair, as she knelt at her feet, and looking down into the sad young face.

There was no sadness in the old lady's; she looked brighter than ever this morning, but, somehow, it was a brightness that made Winny vaguely uneasy, for it was utterly unlike what she feared would follow upon the news of the archbishop's imprisonment, and she looked at the faded old face very lovingly and tenderly as she whispered, " No one shall ever take me from you."

"Bless you, sweetheart, for all your love, and you must tell your father I am very thankful to him for leaving you with me a little longer. I'm wearing away, Winny. This world is too much for me. I cannot understand it, as I thought I could. So many good men are on the wrong side, and so many unworthy ones where all should be true and brave. Master Fuller has been telling me something of his life at Oxford, and how he was as glad to leave the cavalier camp as he had been to escape from London. I would that the king had such men about him as my nephew, Harry Vane, and some others of the Parliament men; then there would be more hope of peace for this distracted realm. We must pray for peace, my Winny," concluded the old lady, for at this moment Dr. Fuller came in to read the prayers and lessons for the day, which Dame Meredith never omitted reading for herself or having read to her.

No questions had been asked Winny about her father and the part he was likely to take in the national quarrel, and she hoped that when he came no mention would be made of this painful topic. It may be that Winny was needlessly anxious about this now, for in truth Dame Meredith had greatly changed within the last few days. The things of earth were shrinking away from her as she approached nearer the heavenly city; and she could even think calmly of the archbishop's imprisonment, and believe, with Dr. Fuller, that God was well able to take care of his Church and of his servant too.

But if Winny thought less of the old man shut out from the world in the Tower, it was because other anxieties pressed upon her to counterbalance it. The doings of the rival armies wore another aspect after her father had left her, and every day she walked down to the high-road to watch for the king's post riding through the village, in the hope of hearing some news of what was going forward at a distance, for here, in lovely Kent, they were far away from the scene of strife.

She often watched and waited in vain, but not always; for her patience was sometimes rewarded by hearing sundry scraps of news, which the post was always liberal in bestowing when he reined in his horse at the village ale-house; and Winny, from the safe shelter of the huge oak where she stationed herself, could hear and see all that passed without herself being seen. Sometimes letters were left for the Vanes or Dame Meredith, and sometimes for herself, for her father divined something of her anxiety on his behalf, and wrote as often as he could safely get a letter conveyed to her.

From the scraps of news thus gathered Winny learned that the royalists were everywhere victorious in the west of England; but, instead of being able to rejoice, as she felt she ought to do, this good tidings only increased her anxiety, until a word came from her father assuring her he was alive and well. Then Winny would breathe more freely for a time, and go about with a less anxious face, until the rumor of another battle reached her; and as she had no means of knowing where her father might be, she, of course, imagined him as being in every battle.

If he had only been fighting on the royalist side every thing would be so different, as she was often whispering to herself; but now her heart was so cruelly divided between her love and loyalty and every principle in which she had been reared, that she could not rejoice and thank God for the conquests of the king, for it might be that this very conquest would throw a dark shadow over all her life.

It was not merely her father's death that Winny lived in such dread of. He would be exposed to the same danger if he had been in the king's army, but Winny would have known nothing of the terrible apprehension she now lived in if he had been fighting on the side of king and holy Church. Nay, if he had been slain under such circumstances she would rather have gloried in him as a martyr of the good cause who had willingly laid down his life in the service of the king.

At last came tidings of the battle of Newbury, where the all-victorious army of the king received its first check, and lost its prince of men—" the glory of the royalist party "—Lord Falkland.

Strange to say, the news of his death affected Dame Meredith more strongly than the imprisonment of the archbishop had done. "Ah me, sweetheart," she sighed ; " peace is further off than ever from this distracted land, now that good man and brave soldier has been taken. Doubtless he was glad of his discharge, for Prince Rupert and the lawless doings of his soldiers were a sore trouble to him ; but I am thinking of the king and this poor bleeding land—no longer 'merry England,' but torn, distracted England, with no hope of healing, now Hampden and Falkland have gone. My poor Winny! your lot is cast in evil times, and I may not see the end of these troubles ; but, my dear, trust steadily in God."

Happily for herself, Dame Meredith was spared the agony of knowing that not only the archbishop but the king was at length imprisoned and condemned to die by those who had taken the helm of affairs at this perilous juncture. It was a very different ending she and Winny had hoped and prayed for, when they pleaded that God would strengthen and build up his Church in righteousness and the beauty of holiness. We know now that these earnest, devout prayers were answered, although it seemed to those who prayed that it was bitterest defeat; for to them the " beauty of holiness " meant what Laud had interpreted it to mean—a mere sensuous worship of splendid ritual, which was gradually choking all true spiritual worship and strangling the life of the Church. God would save her from this even by sore judgment and bitter humiliation, for so it is God often answers the prayers of his servants.

After the defeat of the royalists at Newbury there were a few months of comparative peace, but neither side were idle, for while Harry Vane and the Parliament were negotiating for assistance from the Presbyterians of Scotland, the king was busy arranging for help from the Roman Catholics of Ireland, to renew the struggle at the first favorable opportunity; and during this lull of hostilities Dame Meredith passed away to the land of everlasting peace.

Poor Winny was overwhelmed with grief at the loss of her friend, who had been a mother to her for so many years. It was small consolation to her, either, that she was possessed of an ample fortune, and that a home had been secured for her in the Vane household until her father could claim her.

And so for six months Winny could do little but watch and wait the chances of war, during which time another sore blow fell upon her; for the long-deferred trial against the archbishop was commenced in March, and as it went on it became more certain than ever that he would end his days upon the scaffold. Sorely Winny missed gentle Dame Meredith now. The young Vanes were as hot and passionate in their denunciations of the Parliament, and all who sympathized with them, as Winny had once been, while she—well, she could not understand herself, only she wished she could run to Dame Meredith and hear, as she so often had in her last days, tender, pitiful words, and even excuses made for what had before seemed inexcusable to both of them.

Now her father was one of those whom she had looked upon as enemies, she longed to hear such soothing words again, even though she might herself combat them; but these hard, bitter words of her young companions fell upon her like blows, sometimes causing her the double anguish of doubting her own loyalty, because they pained her so much. And Winny's was not the only heart in which this fierce battle and bitter pain was added to more physical distress. Of this she knew nothing as yet, but she was not long to remain in ignorance of the other side of the gloomy picture.

Early in July came news of a battle fought at Marston Moor, in Yorkshire, and shortly afterward the king's post brought a letter to Winny, written by her brother Rupert, begging her to come at once to their father, who had been sorely wounded fighting with Colonel Cromwell's Ironsides. A messenger was waiting in London to bring her to them without delay, the letter said, and Winny was not long in making her preparations to set out.

In sunny, smiling Kent the fields were waving with corn and the orchards glowed with their harvest of fruit, and London looked as rich and prosperous and busy as ever. But when London was left behind, and they were on the great northern road, they came upon tracts of wilderness and pitiless devastation that made Winny shudder. Wrecks of barns and farm-houses that had once been pleasant homesteads, but now were only heaps of blackened ruins; and what pained her almost as much was to hear that this was the work of Prince Rupert, who would often swoop down upon the inhabitants of a peaceful district with a band of his royalist soldiers, and drive off the cattle and all that could be carried away, and then, if the owners resisted or protested, they were hung to their own door-posts as Puritan traitors, and the house fired.

In this way hundreds of homes in England had been desolated, and the people's heart roused to a hatred against their king such as they had never known before, and which prophesied ill for the success of the royal cause.

What Winny felt about all this she kept close in her own heart, but she was thankful when the journey was over and she was no longer forced to see such cruel sights and hear that all the vaunted chivalry of the cavaliers were as so many idle tales.

She found her father in a less dangerous condition than she feared, although his wounds

were very severe, and he had suffered a good
deal from pain and loss of blood.   Rupert met
her with a half apology for fetching her, for
their quarters were poor and there was little
accommodation for a lady; but Winny quickly
assured him that her greatest wish was to be
at her father's side now Dame Meredith was
dead, and she soon proved that she was no
dainty fine lady unable to do any thing out of
the luxurious home to which she had been
accustomed.

Captain Saxby had been carried to a desert-
ed cottage not far from the scene of the fight,
and although Rubert and the doctor had done
all they could for the comfort of the wounded
man, every thing looked cheerless and desolate in the extreme.

But in a few hours Winny had altered the look
of things in her father's chamber. A few odds
and ends of rough furniture that lay strewed
about the garden were brought in by her brother Rupert, and, cleaned and furbished by Winny, soon gave a more home-like look to the
place, and the wounded soldier seemed to find
a relief from the pain of his wounds and the
monotony of his imprisonment in watching the
graceful figure of his daughter, who was continually busying herself over these small details,

that would never have entered a man's head to contrive.

But when the excitement of her coming was over, and all that could be devised to make the cottage more comfortable had been done, Winny discovered that her father was going back to the same state of listless brooding he had indulged before she came, and she resolved to ask her brother, who was still with them, if he knew of any cause for this. The brother and sister, so long parted, had got used to each other again by this time, and all the old love seemed to have revived, in spite of the difference of opinion existing between them—a difference that was a bitter pain to both, and yet which helped to convince each how much might be said for the opposite side.

"Something on his mind," repeated Rupert when his sister told him about her suspicions.

"Yes, it is something about Uncle Roger, I feel sure," said Winny; "for I heard him say, 'Roger, Roger,' several times in his sleep this morning.

"Hush, hush; yes, it is that, I am afraid," admitted Rupert. "Uncle Roger was fighting in the royalist army, and he and our father met on the battle-field and recognized each

other.   It was not the first time they met
since father had returned to England ; but
they had parted in anger because he refused
to admit father's claim to a share of Saxby,
and to secure it entirely for himself he took
up the royalist cause.   They never met again
until this battle of Marston Moor, and Uncle
Roger has been killed.   We did not mean to
let father know it just now, but some one
spoke of it incautiously, and he overheard
what was said.   But do you know, Winny, we
shall have to move from here soon ?" added
Rupert.

"But can father be moved?" said Winny,
anxiously.

"The doctor says he will never get better
here, and advises his being taken to his native
place, Great Kimble.   Will you talk to him
about it, and try to find out what he thinks of
the plan ?"

To every body's surprise the invalid caught
eagerly at the suggestion, and arrangements
were at once made to have him conveyed in a
litter, and by easy stages, to the village among
the chalk hills where he had played as a boy,
and which he had left five and twenty years
before to fight for freedom and religious liberty.

Rupert hoped that the dear familiar scenes surrounding their ancestral home might soon do all that the doctor thought they would. But, alas, the destroyer had reached Saxby before them, and nothing remained of the old house but a charred heap of blackened ruins, while over fields and orchards desolation and destruction reigned complete.

" It is enough," said the invalid when he caught sight of the ruin ; "take me away as far as you can. I have looked my last at dear old Saxby, that has cost me my brother's life and my father's banishment. Take me to my father now, children. Thank God, his old eyes will never see this mournful sight ! Take me to New Saxby, Rupert, about which you have told me so much. I would fain see my father once more before I die."

From this time his one wish was to see his father, and so, as soon as he was sufficiently recovered from his wounds to be able to travel, the three set out on their voyage to the New England that was henceforth to be their home ; and here Winny learned to understand that the Church of God might include many who did not worship him after a pattern set by kings and bishops, while many a Puritan learned to think more kindly of those who

20

differed from themselves by a visit to the gentle royalist maiden living at New Saxby; for Winny never gave up her love of king and country, and no one ever thought of asking her to do so.

The success of Oliver Cromwell and the establishment of the Commonwealth in England carried the Reformation a step further; but this was followed by a retrograde movement when Charles II. came to the throne from which his father had been hurled; his accession sent many to the New England that was now growing to be a might and power in the world—the home of liberty, the refuge of brave, true souls, who loved liberty more than ease or life itself.

The efforts and prayers of the Pilgrim Fathers who had first set foot on the western wilds had been wonderfully answered. They had said, " If it please God to discover some place unto us, even though in America, where, free from antichristian bondage, we may retain our names and nationality, and not only become a means of enlarging the dominions of the English State, but the Church of Christ also, in that place we will joyfully establish ourselves; and our persecuted countrymen shall see how in the distant wilderness men may comfortably subsist, and keep their consciences unsullied;" and in little more than thirty years, under their vigorous leadership, a New England had arisen; and we trust and pray that the mighty empire born of the Puritans' efforts and prayers will ever be true to her noble lineage, and faithfully keep the priceless trust committed to her by the grand old men of the " Mayflower.

THE END.

www.ingramcontent.com/pod-product-compliance
Lightning Source LLC
Chambersburg PA
CBHW031032120726
47905CB00007B/2157